Web [illegible] Lies

Sheila Hall

Michael Terence
Publishing

First published in paperback by
Michael Terence Publishing in 2021
www.mtp.agency

ISBN 9781800941434

This book is dedicated to the memory of my loving son, Christopher, who left me with so many happy memories.

Introduction

There was a loud banging on the front door. Cathie rushed to answer it, and as she opened the door, an out-sized woman stepped over the doorstep and smacked her right across the face.

"That's to make sure that you keep that brat of a son of yours in check. He has just hit our Johnny. If he touches him again, I'll have the law on you." Cathie reeled back, too stunned to speak. She had never encountered such rough behavior from a woman. She pushed her back over the doorstep and slammed the door shut. Then she slid to the floor in a heap and burst into tears.

Cathie was thirty-seven years old. She had never come across violence before. She had a friendly nature, always willing to help anyone in trouble. She did struggle in this place, however. She found it to be a very hostile environment, totally alien to her upbringing on a quiet farm deep in the North Wales countryside.

The house she had been reallocated to, when she had lost her family home, was on a rough housing estate. It was a transient place where there was no community spirit. It was situated miles from the nearest town and everyone seemed to be waiting for a more suitable place to live. No one seemed to take any pride in their homes by what Cathie had noticed. Dirty curtains, old cars scattered about the streets and gardens full of old cookers, television sets and other accumulated piles of rubbish.

Cathie was a trained nurse, having left the farm when she left school and had decided to join the Army and travel. She left the

Army after she got married. Life had been good in the beginning but now here she was, living in an environment where drugs were bought and sold openly. There was no police presence and hostile teenage gangs roamed the streets. Cathie lay awake most nights, thinking of how she had got into this mess but more importantly thinking of the safety of her children and trying to think of a way to get them away from this awful place. She had been living like this for twelve months now and getting out of bed and facing the day was becoming harder and harder.

I swear if it were not for the children to keep me on the right track I would have taken to the bottle by now, she muttered to herself as she sat there sobbing.

*****

"Whatever is the matter Mam?" cried Sarah, emerging from the kitchen. "What are you doing sitting there? Who was at the door?" Cathie blew her nose and got up off the floor.

"It was some rough old sort," she replied, "I've never seen her before, but I'll remember her in future. She claimed our Neil had hit her son. Our Neil would never start a fight. She must have got him mixed up with another lad. He hasn't got a violent bone in his body. Go and see if you can find him will you Sarah love, but only go to the end of the street. If you do not see him, come back and we'll all go and look for him."

Little Paul was sat watching the television and playing with his dinky cars, totally oblivious to the discussion going on in the hall. Cathie went into the front room and plonked herself down on the worn-out settee and held her arms out to Paul, her little innocent four-year-old. Her children gave her so much comfort in these dark days. Paul clamboured up on to her knee and snuggled up to her. He started running the dinky cars up and down her leg. She giggled.

"You're tickling me." Paul did it all the more as he saw it made his mother laugh.

"I'll get off then Mam," called Sarah grabbing her coat. "I won't be gone long."

"No further than the end of the street, and mind how you go," called Cathie.

"I'll go and call him, I don't expect he is far away, then we'll come home and I will make you a nice cup of tea." She kissed her Mam. Cathie smiled and hugged Sarah.

"You are only eleven but you are such a sensible grown-up girl. I suppose you have had to be. I don't know what I would do without you." She gave Paul another hug. How had she managed to get to this stage in her life? She had lost her home and most of her belongings. And what was more to the point how was she going to get out of it.

*****

Fourteen years previously Cathie had thought that the world could not have been a happier place. She was coming up to her fourth year in the Army, having signed up for student nurse training and had worked hard, qualified as a State Registered Nurse and had achieved the rank of a staff sergeant. They were exciting times. Joining the Army had led her to meet all sorts of interesting people. She had met a girl on the train down to Aldershot and she was now one of Cathie's long-term friends.

Hope she never finds out how low I have sunk. Cathie shuddered. She thought back to more pleasant times. The PTS. (preliminary training school) was daunting. She had to deal with the regimented hours, the marching, under the eagle eyes of the staff sergeant, and the restrictive social hours. Cathie remembered having to be in the billet for twenty-one fifty-nine hours each night except Saturdays when she would have freedom until twenty-two fifty-nine hours. Most of her Saturday nights were spent down at the NAAFI Club. There were plenty of soldiers willing to pay for drinks, but she soon learned to stay within the safety of the club and return to the barracks with her friends. One or two of the girls did skip out again after bed check and go over the fence into town but if you were caught you would be sent home. She didn't want to take the chance and go home to her village in disgrace.

After completing her preliminary training Cathie remembered looking eagerly at the postings board and finding out to her disappointment that she would not be on her way to some exotic posting, but she was being sent to Millbank hospital in London to start her training. It was just off the King's Road in Chelsea. She smiled to herself as she fondly remembered London, Carnaby Street and all the sightseeing trips with her new companions on her days off.

She and her friends made their clothes in those days, as they were paid very little as students. Bed and board and a few pounds a week. Followers of Carnaby Street fashion, they made gaudy-coloured miniskirts and attempted evening dresses for the camp dances. One of the student nurses and a special friend, Liza, had studied dressmaking at college before joining the Army and everyone was very impressed with the help she gave with the sewing projects. Cathie still kept in touch with her. Liza had taken herself off backpacking a couple of years ago and had met and married a sheep farmer in New Zealand. She wouldn't be back any time soon.

Cathie brought herself back to reality.

Just as well. I would be so ashamed to invite her here. The sooner we get out of this place the better.

After a year' training in London, Cathie was delighted to find out she had a posting to British Military Hospital Singapore. This would give her a lot more experience, she thought. After a round of vaccinations and she had been given her tropical kit she was on her way. She grew to love Singapore. Lots of off duty sunbathing, swimming and endless parties. But also, she took her nursing very seriously and studied hard. She gained experience in the isolation ward, the children's ward and working in theatre. She even got to work on the baby unit which she loved. She nursed the sick and injured coming from the war in Borneo and it was one of these soldiers from the Second Battalion, The Parachute Regiment that changed her path in life.

If only I had stuck to the rules. I might not be in this mess now. Almost immediately she regretted her angry feelings. *'You would not have three precious children if you hadn't met Tom,* she convinced herself.

She had been debating making the Army her career and becoming an officer after she had qualified. One thing was holding her back. An Army career and family and children was not an optional choice. Once a nurse got pregnant in the Army she had to leave, married or otherwise, and she did want a family. As she looked down at her little son, she knew she had made the right decision.

*****

Her thoughts wandered back again to those carefree days. No ties, no worries. The Army looked after its own. She had been given a dream posting for two years at the military hospital in Singapore. Whilst in Singapore she had met the man she wanted to spend the rest of her life with. There was no shortage of men to date but there was something about Tom that attracted her especially. She had broken the golden rule and had got involved with one of her patients.

Tom Blackwood was a corporal in The Second Battalion the Parachute Regiment. He had been admitted to hospital following a back injury and severe burns to his legs when his jeep turned over and caught fire whilst out on patrol in Borneo. He was on her ward for several weeks and whilst there he kept up the morale with his endless banter. His injuries didn't seem to affect him. He was a tonic to all the injured men on the ward. He made Cathie laugh and when he was discharged back to his unit, he wrote to her and they started seeing one another. She smiled to herself as she remembered those hedonistic days, full of fun and laughter. It seemed so long ago now. So much had changed.

When she was posted back to the UK, she and Tom would write to each other every other day. She still kept those love letters in a box on the top of her wardrobe. When she felt low, she would get them down and read them. They were very precious to her. Many of the letters contained poems. He had borne his soul in those letters. How could he have changed so much?

Her work took up her time and soon eighteen months had passed and Tom had done his tour of duty in Borneo and was back in Aldershot. He would come up to London to see her on his weekend passes and stay at the Union Jack Club. They had such fun sightseeing around London and going to shows in the west-end. They were very much in love. Tom proposed to

Cathie one hot summers evening. He had come up to meet her after her shift. Flamboyant as ever, she remembered. He had gone down on one knee outside the gates to her billet. Cathie had no doubts in her head whatsoever that this was the man she wanted to marry and be the father of her children. She had been waiting for this moment and nodded eagerly.

"We'll have a dozen kids. We'll be so happy together, my darling." Tom had got up off his knees and was dancing around her. Cathie had reservations about giving birth to twelve children but she caught Tom's mood and threw her head back and laughed.

"We'll be so happy forever and ever." She grabbed hold of him and arms around each other they made their way to her billet.

"Mustn't let the duty sergeant catch you this side of the gate Tom," Cathie giggled. "She'll have a fit if she sees a man in here. I hate to have to go but I must go in or I'll be on a charge. I'll see you tomorrow."

"Can't wait and I love you so much," said Tom.

"Love you too," answered Cathie as they kissed goodnight. She waited on the billet steps until he was out of sight and then went inside to see who was about.

If I have lost Tom, I will never lose those memories. Her mind shot back to those heady days.

She couldn't wait to break the news to any of the nurses who were still up and about.

"Congrats Cathie," said her friend Mandy, when she heard. "I like Tom, he is always so cheerful."

"He makes me laugh, Mandy. That is so important in my book. Better than drop-dead good looks. But I am lucky. Tom is tall, handsome and with a wacky sense of humour."

"You'll not sleep tonight but we better make an effort. We are both on earlies in the morning." Mandy hugged her friend and disappeared into her room. Cathie could not sleep that night and sat in the kitchen for the next hour dreaming of the perfect future that lay ahead.

They were married twelve months later in the Welsh village where Cathie had spent her youth growing up on her parent's farm, attending the local village school and the church on Sundays. The villagers had known her most of her life and they had turned out in force to witness the happy day. Tom's parents and his two sisters had come over from Belfast and were staying in the local pub where the reception would be held later that afternoon.

Cathie arrived at the twelfth century Norman church in a Daimler limousine and walked proudly down the aisle on the arm of her father. Tom and Cathie smiled at one another, knelt in front of the altar and made their solemn vows to be faithful, to love and to care for one another forever. Cathie's eyes filled with tears as she remembered that poignant moment that was filled with hopes and dreams, now shattered and broken and gone forever.

*****

Tom and his best man looked resplendent in their dark blue number one dress uniforms. Cathie wore a white empress style wedding gown and her proud father walked beside her down the aisle. She was attended by three bridesmaids and her sister

Jenny as matron of honour. The bridesmaids were her longtime friends who had joined up and trained to be nurses alongside her. Friends forever, they had pledged. Marion, the bubbly girl from Newcastle, Eliza, a beautiful sophisticated girl from Devon and Anne the quiet, practical one. All nurses now, working in different military hospitals but had come together to celebrate the wedding. They wore bridesmaids' dresses in a burgundy colour and carried sprays of cream carnations to complement Cathie's bouquet of red roses sprinkled with lily of the valley.

As the procession moved down the aisle and out of the church, they passed under a guard of honour arch of crossed swords, as some of Tom's friends from the regiment had also attended the wedding.

It was a lovely day and Tom and Cathie decided to walk the short distance to the reception. The villagers had anticipated this and the newlyweds were showered with confetti and rice as they made their way to The Pheasant Inn. The day would have special memories for a long time for everyone in the village. It was the first time a military wedding had been celebrated in the village since the war.

Cathie sat cuddling Paul and reminiscing about that perfect day. The photograph of the happy couple sat on the mantelshelf. Cathie remembered her vows as if it were yesterday. She wondered sceptically if Tom remembered them also. Perhaps they didn't mean as much to him. But whatever had happened and whatever happened in the future, no -one could take away those memories of her perfect wedding day.

She sniffed as an involuntary tear trickled down her face.

"Don't cry Mummy," whispered Paul. She wiped her eyes

and looked at him.

"I am fine, darling. As long as I have you, children, I will be fine. Come on, let's go and see what's in the cupboard for tea."

Just then the back door opened and Sarah came in with Neil trailing behind her. He was sporting a swollen and cut lip.

"I see you didn't get it all your way then?" Cathie was angry. "Why can't you keep out of trouble. You'll be bringing the police to our door next. Aren't things bad enough without you making things worse? What happened anyway and I want the truth?" Neil glared at her in defiance.

"That low life Johnny was bad-mouthing our Dad. I just had to hit him to shut him up. I didn't want everyone hearing a pack of lies. He soon shut up when I belted him. I only hit him once and when I was walking away his brother punched me in the mouth. I just carried on walking Mum honest. I don't want trouble here either."

"Alright, I believe you, but keep away from that family in future. Mrs. Davies next door did warn me about them. They have been on this estate for ages. The council are reluctant to move them as everywhere they go, they cause trouble. This is the third estate they have been on. Go and clean yourself up Neil, and bathe that swollen lip in cold water and I'll put some T.C.P. on it. It will soon heal. Tea will be on the table in ten minutes. No-one is going anywhere this evening. We will just stay in and have a bit of peace for once."

Later that evening, when the children were settled in bed, Cathie poured herself a glass of wine and turned once more to the wedding photograph on the mantelshelf, then reached up and put it in a drawer. She spoke sharply to herself.

What is the point of pining over what you had? You can never get those times back. Get a hold of yourself and start planning a future for the children, far away from this place. She made a mental note to ring her sister Jenny in the morning but for this evening she couldn't help thinking about the past and remembering happier times.

As she poured out a second glass of wine her thoughts drifted back to the days just after their marriage. Tom had two more years left to serve. They lived in married quarters in South London. It was a big estate and they had a good social life there. Cathie loved to cook and entertain and they had a large circle of friends. The wives were all good company and they were always in one another's houses for coffee and gossip when the men were away on exercise.

When Cathie had completed her service, she had previously made her mind up not to sign on again and with some regrets, said her goodbyes to Army life and took a job at a local hospital. Tom in the meantime had requested an attachment to a training corps so he could learn a trade before leaving the Army. He had always been interested in mechanics and was pleased to have been accepted in the Royal Electrical and Mechanical Engineers. He came home at weekends and life was pretty good.

She sighed as she remembered this honeymoon period in her life and after fourteen months to add to their happiness, Cathie discovered that she was pregnant. They were overjoyed. Now they had to think long and hard about their future. Tom was coming to the end of his training course and after spending maternity leave with her baby, Cathie was reluctant to go back to work and leave him in child care. She wanted to spend every precious moment with little Neil.

*****

Cathie's younger sister Jenny lived in North Wales. When she heard that Tom and Cathie were looking for a house to buy, she saw an opportunity to see more of Cathie. She missed her sister. Following Jenny and Mick's marriage, things had become a bit overcrowded at Mick's parents' house. Jenny and Mick had been allowed to rent a little smallholding. Jenny thought they could make some money to add to the wages Mick brought in if she managed the smallholding. But now she might be able to persuade her sister to come and live nearby. It was an opportunity for Jenny not to feel so isolated and lonely.

'You will be able to buy a house easily up here Cathie,' Jenny wrote in her letter. 'Property is half the price it is in London. And Wales is a lovely place to bring up children. And little Neil could play here on the smallholding with Anne and Dilys. We could even get a pony.' It had all sounded so convincing and at this moment when Cathie was facing an uncertain future, she thanked the Lord that she had her sister living nearby.

Over the years since she had come to Wales, Cathie was so wrapped up in her own idyllic family life, she had not fully understood just how unhappy Jenny was. She now regretted not spending more time with her sister. It was not until Cathie had her marriage problems that Jenny had confided in her totally about the state of her own marriage. Now, at last, they could support one another.

*****

Jenny was Cathie's younger sister by two years. She always felt a bit inadequate against her older sophisticated sister. She had never had the opportunity to study for a career. As a young girl, she had visions of becoming a teacher but when she was sixteen, she fell in love with a boy from the village. Mick had a bad reputation even then. He came from a big family of eleven children and the father had never worked to support his family. His mother looked worn out and lately, it was rumoured in the village, she had taken to the bottle in a big way. Not that anyone blamed her, was the consensus of opinion. With a bone-idle husband and a brood of children to clothe and feed and not one of them lifting a finger to help her around the house. She was just drinking to blot out her unhappy existence. Mick had left school at fifteen and went from job to job. He always ended up arguing with his fellow workers and then just walked off the job. His weekends were spent drinking with his mates and usually ended up in a fight by the end of the night. He wasn't particularly good looking and always had a chip on his shoulder. He never smiled or laughed. What Jenny saw in him Cathie would never know. Their parents warned her not to get serious with him. He was a bad lot. This seemed to make Jenny all the more determined to go out with him.

Cathie remembered the conversation.

"Everyone is scared of him, Cathie. I am so proud that he has chosen me over all the other girls in the village, to be his girlfriend."

"Is that a good thing?" queried Cathie. "He is no more than a thug and one who drinks too much at that." It was not what Jenny wanted to hear.

"You sound just like Mum and Dad," she protested. "Anyway," she confided. "We have gone all the way now. He said he wants to marry me."

"You fool Jenny. We promised one another we would not do it with any boy until we were married. You are just a kid. He won't have any respect for you now."

"Don't tell Mum and Dad, will you?" pleaded Jenny.

"You are stupid, our Jenny. I will keep your secret but do be careful. Make sure he uses those French letters."

Within three months the inevitable happened. Cathie caught the end of the conversation as she came through the door.

"How could you Jenny? You have just put an end to all your hopes of becoming a teacher and for what? To end up with that waster. You have disappointed your mother and me." Her mother had been crying but she sniffed and looked at Jenny.

"You don't have to get married you know. We can bring up your baby and you could still go to college. We don't want you getting mixed up with that Mick or his family. They are all as rough as one another and none of them has ever done a day's work in their lives."

"Mother is right. We will help you all we can. Don't get married to that lout, Jenny, please." Her father was making a big effort to stay calm. Jenny was sat in the corner by the fire with her head down. She looked so young and unhappy, Cathie went over and hugged her sister.

"Think about what Mum and Dad have said, for goodness sake Jenny. Surely you don't want to be married yet? Mick is too young as well. Have you thought about that? He is too young to settle down. He is only seventeen. How is he going to support you and a baby?"

"I love him though, Cathie. I want to be married and have a home of my own with Mick and the baby." Jenny was adamant.

"Heaven help you, Jenny, if that is what you want," retorted her father. "We won't give our permission for you to marry him.

You know that don't you?" Her father was beginning to lose his temper. "What other parents would offer to look after the baby? You would probably be kicked out on to the street or put in a home for unmarried mothers." Jenny started to cry and ran up to her bedroom.

"I'll go after her Mum," said Cathie. Her parents looked at one another in despair.

"We want to be together, Cathie. Mick is so excited about the baby and we have talked about what we are going to do. Mick is going to get a job on the building site where those new houses are going up and we can live at his parents for now until we can rent somewhere. They have told us that. He has promised me he will give up the drink. He said he wanted to be at home with me and the baby at night, not down the pub."

How naïve and vulnerable my little sister was then. She was only a child and soon to become a mother. I only wish I knew then what I know now. She put up with such a lot after she was married. She is the strong one and I should stop feeling sorry for myself. With that resolve firmly planted in her mind, there was no more going back now for Cathie. She recalled all the past mistakes and was determined to build a better future for the children, Jenny and herself.

*****

"Please try to make Mum and Dad understand, Cathie. I will be all right. Mick and I will be happy. He has promised to look after me."

"It's just that you are so young, Jenny. You are throwing away any chance of a future for yourself. Mum and Dad wanted us to learn to stand on our own two feet and have careers before getting married. It has come as a big shock to them. They still see you as their little girl. I will speak to them but what if they refuse to permit you to marry? You are under age you know."

Jenny had made up her mind.

"I will go and live with his parents anyway and they will have to go to court to get me back. I know they would not like that scandal. I have brought enough on them now. Better to just let us marry and have done with it."

"Yes, you certainly have stirred up a hornet's nest, haven't you? You have not given a minute's thought to what you have done to Mum and Dad. I will talk to them and I hope you don't live to regret your actions."

Within two months Mick and Jenny were married at the register office in the town. It was a very hushed affair, not the kind of wedding that her parents had envisaged for her. The two sets of parents hardly spoke to one another. Cathie was a witness alongside one of Mick's brothers. They went over to the pub after the ceremony and after a buffet and a toast to the bride and groom, Mick, Jenny and his parents made their excuses and left. Cathie still remembered the look of hurt on her mother's face as Jenny left with her new in-laws.

Cathie recalled the day she approached Tom with the idea of moving to Wales. She liked the idea of moving closer to her sister. At this time, she had no idea that Jenny was so unhappy. She wanted to move for the reasons her sister had suggested. A lovely area in the countryside to bring up children. Cathie herself had attended a village school and had memories of a very happy childhood. Walks in the snow in winter, picking bluebells in the spring, summer picnics, climbing trees, playing with the dogs on the fields. She wanted the same opportunities for her Neil. Tom was in total agreement as he had also been brought up in a small village in County Down in Northern Ireland.

Chapter One

As soon as Tom was discharged from the Army they drove up to Wales and stayed in a holiday cottage whilst they hunted for property and soon found the ideal place. A rambling Victorian house with a large garden for Neil to play in, about two miles from Jenny's smallholding.

Life was quiet for Cathie and Tom after the hustle and bustle of Army life and they took time to adjust. They spent a couple of months painting and decorating and furnishing their new house and sorting out the garden. Every Sunday they would drive over to visit Jenny. Mick was usually out and Jenny seemed so pleased to see them and catch up with their news. Neil loved playing out in the fields with his cousins.

"Mick out again, is he?" Tom enquired casually one Sunday. Jenny was on the defensive.

"He has gone over to his parents to help his Dad with something. He will probably be back soon." Cathie hoped he would stay away all afternoon. She did not like her brother-in-law. There was something about him. He was too plausible with her.

"Shifty eyes," she remarked to Tom later. "He does not look directly at you. It's as if he's hiding something."

"You are just trying to find fault because you don't like the family. He is ok Cathie." She let the matter drop.

Tom and Cathie settled into a routine of married life. Cathie got to know other mothers at the school and they sometimes had a get together in one another's houses for coffee, whilst the children played. Sometimes they would have couples over for dinner parties. They soon had a wide circle of friends and a full social life. Cathie joined the local running club and Tom the darts team at the local pub.

Over the next six years, Cathie and Tom had two more children. Neil was two and a half when Sarah was born then Paul was born five years later. They had always wanted children and now their family was complete. Cathie had managed to persuade Tom that three mouths to feed were quite enough on their income. She still remembered the night when he proposed and his vision of twelve children. Since having the three children Tom had changed his mind and agreed with her.

When they first moved to Wales Tom had got a job working as a mechanic in the local garage and Cathie worked as a part-time night sister at the local hospital. Money was quite tight in those days, she remembered, with the mortgage and three children to clothe and feed but with hindsight how she wished for those days back again. Regular wages coming in. They had managed and they were happy.

She shuddered as she recalled the day Tom had come home all excited and told her he had something to discuss with her. He sounded so enthusiastic. He told her he had heard of a garage for sale.

"I have always wanted to work for myself, you know that Cathie," he began. "It's not only a garage. There is a minibus company to go with it. I have gone over the books and it is a good business, honestly Cathie." He paused for breath and looked at her. Cathie remembered the sinking feeling in the pit of her stomach. It sounded like too much of a commitment to her. Too much of a risk. They had little savings. They would have to borrow a lot of money to buy the garage and would have to put up the house as security. There would be no guaranteed income coming in from Tom. She took a deep breath as all these doubts and worries flashed through her mind. If only she had voiced them and not let her heart rule her head. If only she had been firmer. How many times had she said the words 'If only?

Chapter Two

The day after her wedding Mick began to change and Jenny started to regret what she had done. She hated being stuck up in the box room at Mick's parents' house.

"Most people go on a honeymoon after the wedding," she complained to Mick pulling a face.

"Just be thankful you have a roof over your head and a husband," he sneered. "Most girls in your condition would have been thrown out on to the streets." Jenny was shocked by his attitude.

"But this is your baby. I thought this was what you wanted." Jenny was close to tears.

"Do you think I would have married you if my mother had not wanted her first grandchild? She made me promise to marry you. I had no choice," he snapped back at her. Jenny flopped down on the bed.

"All those loving words and promises. It was just to get me to give in to you, wasn't it? I have been such an idiot. I believed everything you said." She started to cry.

"You can just cut that out an' all or I'll belt you one. I'm going out." And with that remark, Mick clomped down the stairs banging the bedroom door behind him.

Jenny was devastated. She couldn't tell Cathie or her parents. She couldn't bear the words 'I told you so'. She was too proud. She lay on the bed with her arm around her unborn child, staring into space until her mother-in-law called her down for her tea.

Jenny tried hard not to let her situation get her down. She helped her mother-in-law, Mrs. Jones, with the children. She learned how to cook and mend clothes. She was happier when Mick was out of the house, she regretfully admitted to herself.

The night her pains started Mick drove her to the local hospital to have the baby, grumbling all the way that she had interrupted his supper. Jenny was very frightened. It felt like she had a vice around her abdomen and then it stopped and started again. She didn't know quite what to expect. She got no comfort from Mick. He just drove along at a steady pace smoking a cigarette and taking no notice of the distress his wife was in. She had read magazines on childbirth but neither her mother nor her mother-in-law had ventured to tell her very much.

"You will be alright dear," her mother had previously tried to reassure her. "Women have babies every day." And that was all she had told her. Her mother-in-law wasn't much better.

"It's nature, love," she had told her. "Once the child is born all the pain is forgotten. Look at me. If it was that bad women wouldn't have more than one." And that was all the information she could glean out of them. She had not attended any anti-natal classes. Mick told her she didn't need to bother. He had listened to his mother. Giving birth was natural. He didn't see what all the fuss and bother was about. Jenny just accepted their views. It was the easiest way to keep the peace.

When they arrived at the hospital, a porter found her a wheelchair and took her up to the ward. The midwife attending Jenny was very kind and helpful. She shooed Mick out of the ward, drew the screens around Jenny and asked her to get undressed and into bed. After about ten minutes the midwife came back and sat on the bed and went through the birth procedure step by step. She sensed how frightened Jenny was.

"This is women's work," she began. "Men just get in the way. We'll ask your husband to come in when baby arrives." Jenny smiled at her gratefully. By now the pains were getting stronger. She bore her pain bravely, not wanting to make a fuss as Mick might hear her, and in the early hours of the next morning baby Anne was born.

Happy and exhausted Jenny felt an immediate strong surge of love for her helpless little daughter. She had never felt such a strong emotion before. Tired out, she smiled at Mick as he met his daughter. He didn't say much to her and soon left. Jenny had a distinct feeling that Mick had only stayed because the midwife expected him to. Nothing could dampen Jenny's mood. She just smiled in wonder at her beautiful daughter and then she let the nurse take her baby away to the nursery for the night whilst she got some well-earned sleep.

Mick and his parents drove to the hospital the next morning. His mother was beaming with delight at the sight of her first grandchild. Mick and his father were not so enthused.

"Another mouth to feed," grunted his father. Mick bent over the crib.

"Maybe a boy next time," was all he commented. But nothing could curb Jenny's happiness.

"I want to call her Anne after my mother, Mick," she stated.

"Yes, that will do," replied Mick. "Nothing too fussy." He went silent. "We'd better get off, Jenny," Mick stated after about fifteen minutes. "I have a job this afternoon."

"Alright then," replied Jenny, hoping the relief did not sound too obvious. "My Mum and Dad are coming this afternoon so I will have plenty of company.

When she got home after a week of being pampered in the hospital, Jenny found it impossible to get any rest in the little box room with Mick and the baby. She protested to Mick that they would have to find somewhere to rent for themselves. For once Mick agreed with her.

"I have been looking, Jenny. Stop nagging will you. Neither of us is getting any sleep with you up and down all night feeding and changing the baby. And I have to go to work. You can't swing a cat around in here, what with the cot and the bed." Jenny tried to keep Anne as quiet as she could. Mick would get annoyed with her if he got woken up during the night. She did not sleep herself for that reason. She tried to grab a nap when Anne slept during the daytime.

When Anne was about two months old, Mick came in from work one evening and told her he had seen a smallholding for rent.

"You told me once that you would like a place like your Mum and Dads'. It's a bit run down," he explained. "But the landlord said we wouldn't have to put down a deposit if we agreed to do some repairs, so I said we would have it." Jenny's face lit up.

"At last, we will have some space Mick, and Anne can have her own room."

"I thought that would put a smile on your miserable face," answered Mick. "But you will have to tend to the smallholding, mind. And maybe your dad could help with the repairs as I will be out at work for most of the time. The JCB is booked out weeks in advance."

"I will love it, Mick. We will be a proper little family. You remembered what I said about wanting a smallholding. We can get a few sheep and poultry and I can grow our own vegetables. I can't wait." Mick grunted.

"Well as long as it suits you and you won't be nagging me every time I come in. It must be better than being cooped up in here."

Jenny hoped that their situation had turned a corner. It was the first thoughtful gesture Mick had made towards her since their marriage. They moved into the smallholding within a few weeks and life ran a bit smoother for Jenny with all the extra space. Anne had her own bedroom and Jenny painted it a pretty pink and made new curtains. A proper little girl's room.

She soon got on good speaking terms with her neighbours and they helped her obtain a few sheep, half a dozen hens and two geese. She thought that was quite enough to manage as well as Anne and the housework. She was happier than she had been in a long time and any spare time was spent outdoors tending to the animals or her vegetable patch.

The only tension in her life was when she heard Mick's vehicle coming down the drive, and wondering what sort of a mood she would find him in. She couldn't help but feel her stomach churning with fear as soon as she heard his pickup. He had hit her once or twice and she was scared of him. Thankfully, he was away from early morning to evening. Anne was usually in bed before he came home. His job as a JCB driver was well paid and he was bringing in good money.

Anne was eighteen months old when Jenny discovered that she was pregnant again.

"This time it's a boy for sure," commented Mick.

"We don't know that do we," said Jenny tentatively, "but this time I do want to attend the anti-natal classes and see the midwife regularly. I am not going through that again without some medical support, like last time."

"I don't know why not," commented Mick. "Why do you make such a big deal about having a kid? My mother just got on with it." Jenny did not reply. What would be the point? She would get her Dad to take her to the clinic.

As her time grew near, Jenny became extremely anxious. She voiced her worries to Mick's mother.

"Mick has his heart set on a boy. What if it's a girl? He never takes much notice of Anne. I don't know how he would react to another girl."

"I am sure he will love the baby, boy or girl," assured Mrs. Jones. "He just doesn't show his feelings very easily." Jenny had to be content with that.

The baby was born at the local hospital without any complications. A perfect baby girl.

"Go and see them Mick, please," pleaded his mother.

"I am not going and that is that," answered her son banging his fist down hard on the table. "I have no interest in another squawking female brat. I told her I didn't want another girl. They can go to hell as far as I am concerned."

"You are being ridiculous son. I am thoroughly ashamed of you." His father had turned around in his armchair and overheard the conversation above his favourite television show. "No-one can guarantee the sex of a child. You just hope it is healthy. Why can't you just be thankful for that? It certainly isn't Jenny's fault that it's a girl. More like yours. I think the father determines the sex."

"That's rubbish," retorted Mick glowering at his father.

"There is no reasoning with him until he has calmed down," Mrs. Jones remarked to her husband. "What do you know about anything anyway? Well, are we going up to the hospital or not? I want to see our new grandchild." Mick stormed out slamming the door behind him.

When the in-laws visited at the hospital, Jenny wondered if Mick would be with them. As he had not come, Jenny knew in her heart that he wasn't pleased.

"I am going to name her Dilys after you, Mrs. Jones," she informed her mother-in-law. "Where is Mick?" Her in-laws looked at one another.

"You best know the truth love," explained Mrs. Jones. "No use beating about the bush. He won't come and see the baby just yet. He blames you for having another girl. We told him that was rubbish but he's got himself all worked up about it. Best he stays away until he calms down. You know what he's like."

"I knew this would happen," said Jenny, worry written all over her face. "He has been on about having a boy for the last six months. I have never known anyone behave like this." She was near to tears as she looked around the ward at all the proud fathers showering their wives with gifts and admiring their newborns.

"He'll be alright love. He's just disappointed. Give him time," Mrs. Jones remarked patting her hand.

"He needs a boot up his backside." retorted her father. "You have spoilt him, Mother. I am ashamed of him."

Jenny looked at her mother-in-law for a reaction but saw nothing, except a worn-out woman with the weight of the world on her shoulders. It was on the tip of her tongue to tell his mother how Mick would beat her if he came home drunk and how unhappy she was with her bully of a son but she held her tongue. Mick would only take it out on her as soon as he could if his parents found out she had been telling tales.

"I'll get my Mother to stay a while longer," she told them. "She is happy looking after Anne and the animals and hopefully things will settle down," said Jenny none too convincingly.

"That's a good idea," agreed Mrs. Jones sighing. "Mick is a good boy really; he will come round."

Chapter Three

Cathie was so enthusiastic in the early days when the garage business was all new. Tom and Phil, their new full-time driver and assistant mechanic, had gone off to the car auctions one evening. They returned with a second-hand estate car.

"This will be our first project," Tom informed her enthusiastically. "It is nice and roomy for luggage and has not done many miles. We have a spray booth in the garage and when we have finished with her, she will look brand new and we could make a tidy profit on her. What do you think, Cathie?" In those days she only wanted Tom to be happy and nodded in agreement. He was so excited and she felt the mood of excitement also.

"I'm off home now Tom, and see you first thing. My wife will have to get used to me working long hours till we are up and running so best make the most of an early night." Phil was in his forties, and had four children at home and had known Tom for some time.

"I'm glad we have Phil to help us, Tom," Cathie told him after Phil had left. "He is a good worker and won't let us down."

"I' m glad too Cathie. We've got a good one there. Now let's take his advice and get an early night too, although I probably won't sleep. I am much too excited. I have so many plans racing round in my head."

In due course, they had obtained three more cars to restore and sell on the forecourt. Tom and Phil took it in turns to drive the minibus. Tom had inherited school contracts with the business so there was a regular income coming in alongside doing up the cars. As the locals got to know them, they had a trickle of cars booked in for repairs. They gained a reputation for good workmanship and the business was doing well. They took on a young apprentice called Jimmy. He was a cheeky lad but very keen to become a fully qualified mechanic. He went to the local college in between working at the garage and entertained Tom and Phil with stories of what girls he was dating and how far he had got with them.

"You be careful," Tom warned him. "One of these days you may have another little mouth to feed." Jimmy laughed.

"I'm too careful for that. I am not going to settle down just yet." He started whistling a tune as he drove one of the cars up on to the ramp.

Megan Williams was employed the following month to answer the phone and order car parts when they were needed. It had become too much for Cathie as well as the home and the children and the accounts to take care of, so they took on Megan part-time in the afternoons and Cathie worked at the garage in the mornings when she had dropped the older children at school. Little Paul was still a baby then. She answered the phone and did the wages and accounts in between.

Cathie had taken an instant dislike to Megan. She found her brash and suggestive and was always flirting with the male customers.

"She is nothing but a tart, Tom. She may as well have nothing on her top half most of the time. Don't tell me you haven't noticed." Tom looked bemused.

"She doesn't mean any harm, Cathie. She is just friendly."

"Friendly my eye," retorted Cathie. "Her jeans are so tight it's a wonder they don't split. And have you seen how she leans over the desk to chat with the men who come into the office? They must get an eyeful."

"Well, I haven't heard them complaining Cathie. It's good for business, but don't you try it mind." Tom laughed.

"Well, I feel sorry for her poor husband." Cathie sounded cross that Tom had laughed at her. "I bet she has a convenient friend whom she can stay with overnight if she needs an alibi."

"Oh, that is what you women do is it if you have a mind to stray?" Tom kissed her and carried on back to the garage.

Cathie remembered how hard they had all worked. They had extra money to treat the children. The work contracts were increasing. Life was good. She and Tom enjoyed working together. But for what? She could look back now and realize where they had gone wrong. They had grown too big too quickly. If only they were a bit more experienced. How many people in the world had said that she wondered? With hindsight- but hindsight was not an option. She could hear Tom's voice clearly as she sat there remembering.

"We need another minibus to deal with these contracts. A new factory has just opened up and they want us to collect the staff from the villages. There are no buses to tie in with the shifts. We will get a new minibus. It will pay for itself soon enough. No good buying rubbish." Cathie went cold at the thought.

"We have a good business Tom," she recalled, trying to reason with him. "We are paying our way. Why do we need more contracts? That will mean more staff and more risk to our house. Don't let us borrow any more money please." Tom took little notice, she remembered.

"I don't want rival firms to get these contracts, Cathie. You must see that. The second-hand car trade is slow at the moment. We need the business. It's guaranteed money."

"But we will be borrowing against the house again," Cathie argued. She could hear warning bells. Tom went quiet. She knew she would have to agree with him in the end. That is what she did. They made an appointment to see the bank manager.

"The car trade is a very risky business Tom," advised Mr. Thomas, the bank manager.

"But these contracts are solid. In black and white," protested Tom. "If I don't have another minibus, I can't take them on. You must want our business to grow?" Mr. Thomas scrutinized the papers Tom had given him.

"But these contracts are annual."

"Yes, but they have renewed automatically and have been for the last three years. We always get paid on time, there has never been a problem." Eventually, Tom's enthusiasm won over the bank manager and he agreed to lend Tom and Cathie three thousand pounds against their house.

"Now we can put a deposit on a new minibus and keep the payments up as we get paid. We can take on more work Cathie," said Tom as they made their way back to the garage. "We'll be millionaires before you can say, Jack Robinson." Tom gave her a hug. Cathie tried to be positive.

"Well, if we work as hard as we are doing, we will build a good business for our children's future," she replied as she hugged him back.

If only I had been a bit firmer with him. Cathie sat remembering and turning everything over in her mind for the umpteenth time. *You were so stupid to let Tom persuade the bank manager to lend us all that money against our home. Look where it has got us now. I could kick myself.* That was the beginning of the end for her and Tom. Sadly, she had realized it all too late.

Chapter Four

Following the purchase of the new minibus, little by little the accounts looked less solid. Some of the bills were being put on hold until the following month. Cathie aired her concerns to Tom on many an occasion but Tom was riding on a high. He would not listen. He had complete faith in their success. He just told Cathie to stop worrying. Everything would be alright. But Cathie had been keeping up to date with the news and the word 'recession' kept cropping up. This was a word they were not familiar with but they soon learned what it meant to them. The workforce contracts failed to be renewed as people were getting laid off from the factories due to lack of orders. It was a chain reaction and out of their control. All too soon they realized they had too many debts and overheads relying on their contract work. *It was all such a mess,* Cathie realized.

Tom began to change. He had lost his sparkle and became withdrawn and quiet. He started staying out late down at the Red Dragon, their local pub. Cathie had strong suspicions that there was a woman involved. She knew all the signs from her time spent with the Army wives. She suspected Megan. Now she knew there was more to it than that. *If only it was just that little tart,* she mused. *I can deal with her, but it's more than that I can tell.*

Tom felt as if he was on a never-ending treadmill of self-destruction and unable to stop it and get off. He was worried sick at the beginning of their financial problems. He felt that he was losing his grip on the business. He so wanted to make his family proud of him, but the bills kept piling up. He had known it for the past twelve months but had refused to listen to Cathie's warnings. If he went down to the Red Dragon at night, he would drink heavily to block out his troubles.

The recession had hit them badly. One of the minibuses stood idle in the garage and no-one had any spare money to buy his cars. The council were not renewing as many contracts, as they were making their own cutbacks. Cathie looked serious every time she looked at their accounts.

"It's not working, Tom," she would tell him. "We have to pay out more than is coming in." He would get annoyed.

"Just stop nagging will you. I 'm working as hard as I can, Cathie. It is not my fault. I 'm going out." That was his answer to the problem every time. He just refused to discuss it with her. God, he had been so stupid.

Cathie sighed as she remembered the number of times, she had tried to get Tom to sit down and try to work out a way to get out of the financial mess they were slipping into.

Tom stormed out of the house and made his way to the pub. He knew he would find a solace there to forget his troubles for a while.

"Hiya Tom," he heard a familiar voice. Megan was sat at the bar with some of the regulars. "Come and sit by me," she called. Tom had been fending her off for about twelve months. He was not interested. She was attractive, he had to admit but loud with it. He didn't like the way she dressed. Tight skirts and low-cut blouses. Always flirting with men. Tom was sure she had had affairs with one or two of the married men who frequented the garage. She was usually in the pub without her husband. He was the total opposite of her. Tom knew him. A quiet man who liked to stay at home, spending most of his spare time doing up bikes in his garden shed and selling them through advertising in the local paper.

"You look tired, Tom," Megan persisted and moved to sit by him. She put her hand on his knee and started to move her hand up and down his leg. "Come and sit in a more comfortable place and I will get you a drink." He smiled at her. He needed a bit of comforting. Perhaps she was just lonely, he justified his actions. He could welcome a sympathetic ear.

"Thanks, Megan, get one for yourself." At that particular moment, he was just grateful for some female attention that did not involve money worries.

"I'll just have the one and then I must get on home," Tom informed her.

"All right, love," she agreed, knowing full well that Tom always said that, but in his present mood he would stay till the pub closed and even later if the landlord had a lock-in. Gradually Tom had to admit to himself that he had begun to find some comfort in Megan's company but up to now he had stopped short of any involvement with her.

"We are just friends, you must understand that, Megan," he told her. "I am a happily married man. I love my wife." Megan pouted.

"They all say that," she laughed.

"You have a husband, Megan,"

"Some husband he is," retorted Megan. "One of these days he might come out of the bike shed and remember that he's got a wife." Tom wondered if her husband was still putting up with her affairs or if they had split up altogether.

As the weeks went by and the business did not improve, Tom spent more and more of his evenings down at the pub. Cathie spent more and more time pouring over the accounts and wondering if her husband was being unfaithful with that blowzy tart, Megan. She had heard some rumours. She and Tom had been arguing a lot lately and it usually ended with him storming off and disappearing for hours. She had begun to check his pockets for anything suspicious, something she had always despised and vowed she would never do, but Tom was either extra careful or innocent. She couldn't decide which. She did not want to confront him until she had absolute proof of an affair. She was very unhappy. She toyed with the idea of confiding in her sister but held back out of loyalty to Tom. After all, she had no proof.

Chapter Five

Tom recalled one particular night. Down at the Red Dragon, Tom's brother-in-law Mick walked in. He had obviously had a few pints already from the look of him. He made a beeline for Tom.

"Can't you stand the sight of your missus either?" he grinned. "I heard you were spending a lot of time down here." He glanced at Megan. "I see you have company." He looked slyly at Tom.

"It's not what you think, Mick," replied Tom. "We are not all like you."

"If you say so," answered Mick not looking at all convinced.

Tom was well aware that Mick had been with a string of women since his marriage. He had not told Cathie as he knew Mick would never change and would probably take revenge out on Jenny if he was confronted, so he kept his mouth shut and told himself it was none of his business.

Mick was curious to know why Tom was not at home with Cathie and the kids. Spending time with another woman was totally out of character. He knew how easy Megan was. He had been with her himself and did not doubt in his mind that Tom was having an affair. He knew the signs. He liked Tom and Cathie and thought they were happy together. Tom was easy going and never interfered in his and Jenny's sham of a marriage. Mick was not of the same mind. He wanted to know the ins and outs and why his brother -in-law's marriage had suddenly taken a wrong turn. He started to come to the pub regularly when he thought Tom would be there.

"Are you spying on me?" Tom asked him one evening. Tom was sitting on his own. "Not all of us are like you, Mick. After every bit of skirt, you can get your hands on. I just feel sorry for Jenny."

"Oh her," replied Mick. "She knows all about me. She doesn't care what I do or who I see as long as I bring home the wages. All she cares about is working on that smallholding and seeing to the kids. She has no time for me."

"Well, you've never really tried, have you, Mick? She would be better off without you." Mick nodded.

"I totally agree and one of these days she will get her wish and I'll be off." He seemed relieved that someone would listen to the reasons he had ended up so unhappy. He had forgotten that he wanted to find out about Tom's problems.

"I feel so trapped Tom, I always have," he began. The drink was loosening Mick's tongue. "I feel as if I am drowning sometimes. I dream of getting away, seeing the world. I have never been anywhere. You have seen places before you got married. Some lads I know have just gone to work in Australia. All that sun and sand. I wish to God I had never got Jenny pregnant. It's like a millstone around my neck. I never wanted kids."

Tom was quite shocked. He couldn't imagine a world without his children in it. "I never knew you felt like that Mick," he said. "Is that what makes you such a miserable bastard at home?"

"Probably," agreed Mick. "Do you want another pint?"

Tom and Mick saw one another more regularly, spending their evenings drinking together. It was a good excuse for Tom to shake off Megan. She had serious feelings for him, talking about divorce and babies. Tom admitted he had led her on a bit and had promised her many things in the heat of the moment in the back of his car. Now he needed an excuse to cool things off. She was nothing to him, just a bit of fun when he was feeling down. He encouraged Mick to spend time with him, telling Megan he was helping Mick with his marriage problems.

"That's rich," huffed Megan. "You're a fine one to give out advice on marriage guidance." After a few evenings of realizing that Tom had other things on his mind, she was not one to let the grass grow under her feet and soon set her sights on one of the local factory workers. Tom was relieved and hoped none of his dallying with her had got back to his wife.

Mick talked to Tom a lot about his marriage to Jenny and how unhappy he was. He failed to mention the beatings, only the rows between them. He painted a picture of a very unhappy man, who worked hard to feed his family but was totally unappreciated by his wife, distant from his children and in a place where he didn't want to be. He admitted he sometimes took out his frustrations on his wife, whom he had been forced to marry when they were still no more than children themselves. Mick felt that he was missing out on life.

After two- or three-pints Tom started to see his point of view. He glazed over the womanizing, the rows, and Mick's total lack of interest in his children, or the fact that Mick had got Jenny pregnant in the first place. He was seduced by Mick's whining and of how unhappy he was and how he desperately wanted a new life.

"We're both unhappy Mick, but for different reasons," Tom told him. "I have made a mess of things up to now as well. I love Cathie and the kids. We were doing fine. Now we are in a financial mess and I hope to God she doesn't find out about Megan. I don't know what I was thinking of. A diversion I suppose. We are about to lose our house and Cathie and I do nothing but row over money all of the time. The kids hate us rowing and all I do is come down here for a bit of peace. Mick looked at him.

"I didn't realize things were that bad Tom, and all I do is keep banging on about my problems. It seems to me that we could both do with a heap of money to change both our lives."

"That would certainly be the answer Mick," agreed Tom. "But we are only dreaming. I don't even do the football pools."

Chapter Six

Tom didn't see Mick for a few weeks. He assumed he was with another woman. He tried to keep away from the Red Dragon in case Megan made a beeline for him again. It was a bit awkward if their paths crossed in the garage but he had begged Megan to keep her mouth shut. She had kept quiet up to now, supposedly as she wanted to keep her job. This was one more thing that Tom had to worry about. He promised Cathie he would not waste so much of their income over the bar at the local pub. Cathie was pleased that he was not drinking so much but thought to herself that his efforts were too little too late to make any difference to their situation. They were still keeping their heads just above water but if any payments were missed, they would lose their house. She was desperately worried.

One evening when Cathie had been pouring over the accounts for the umpteenth time, she approached Tom again with her worries.

"We are still in the red Tom," she began. "I don't know how we will be able to meet next month's payments on the mortgage. I will just have to go back to work and you will have to stop in and look after the children. It's the only way." She sounded exasperated. Tom stared at her.

"I am sick and tired of you moaning on about money. And I am not having you go out to work and shaming me. Everyone will know then, that I am unable to look after my family. I can't work any harder than I do. It is not my fault that the factory contract has not been renewed. They are laying people off." He was trying to control his anger and frustration. His voice was getting louder and louder.

"Calm down Tom," Cathie said quietly. "You will upset the children. Can't we sit down together and try to work out where we can cut corners."

"We have done that time and time again Cathie. I'm up to here with it," he shouted pointing at his forehead. "I don't want to discuss it anymore. I'm off out where I can forget your nagging for a few hours."

With that, he stormed out slamming the door behind him. Neil was in the other room and had overheard everything.

"I wish I could help, Mum," he said. Can't I get a part-time job?" Cathie smiled fondly at him.

"In a couple of years darling," she replied. "We may be glad of a hand then. You are only twelve. A hundred years ago we could have sent you out to work but thank goodness things have changed since then. You need to concentrate on your schooling and pass your exams. It's me who should be bringing in a wage but your Dad won't hear of it. Now don't worry. It's only money. Things will get better. You kids are worth more to me than all the money in the world." She hugged him tightly.

Tom later recalled how he had got into his car that night and had driven off, screeching his tyres in temper. He parked up in the Red Dragon car park and sat there in despair.

I'll get one of the lads to drop me off home tonight. I'll leave my car here. I am in the mood to get hammerered. I've just about had enough of worrying about money and I'm sick of myself. It's all my fault, getting us into this mess. Me and my big ideas I wouldn't listen to Cathie or the bank manager.

I knew best. I know I have to find a way to get us back on track but I just need one night to forget all about it. After his pep talk to himself, he went up to the bar and ordered a whisky. As he was ordering his drink Mick strolled in with some woman Tom had never seen before. Mick sat her down and joined Tom at the bar.

"Hi Tom, you're not usually here on a Tuesday night. I wouldn't have brought Norma in if I'd have known you'd be here. I'll get rid of her."

"I don't care what you do," replied Tom. "I've got bigger things to worry about than seeing you cheating on my sister-in-law. That's your business."

"I'll get rid of her anyway," replied Mick. "You look as if you could do with some company." He walked over to Norma and told her he had family business to see to and they would have to make it another night. She looked peeved.

"Do what you like Mick," she told him. "You're not much company anyway. I'll see you around maybe." And with that remark, she flounced out of the pub.

"I'll grab us a table," said Mick. "Bring the drinks over, she's gone now." This was Tom's second mistake.

They sat down and started to talk about things in general, the weather, the garage, whether things were any better between Mick and Jenny, the children. Anything but the subject Tom was bursting to share with someone.

After about four pints Tom started to open up and tell Mick what had happened that evening.

"Things are no better financially," he admitted to Mick. "I can't seem to find a way out of it."

"I am surprised," Mick told him, "I know you told me you were having money worries but I thought it was just a blip and you were on the up. I had visions of you being a millionaire one day Tom. You are always expanding the business." Tom laughed.

"It's all borrowed money, Mick. And borrowed against the house as security. I wouldn't listen to Cathie that we were taking too much of a gamble. We may lose the house and the business or even worse, go bankrupt."

Mick swore and sucked in his breath. "You can't let that happen, Tom. Cathie would never forgive you. She would leave you and take the kids. You'd be left on your own."

"I know, I know." Tom put his head in his hands. "I don't know what to do."

Mick went quiet for a while.

"Look, Tom, you seem pretty desperate and I do trust you. I have been chewing over a way of getting hold of some cash myself. Just don't want to do it on my own. I need money too. Between you and me I plan to get away. I was trapped into marriage. I had planned to travel to Australia and backpack my way around the country. All that went up in the air when Jenny told me she was pregnant. I was seventeen for God's sake. Not done anything or been anywhere. As I've mentioned before, she doesn't need me. I am just a wage packet and the social would provide that. She is quite happy digging away on the smallholding and I hardly ever see the kids. They would all get along a lot better if I was off the scene. Jenny and I are at each other's throats most of the time. We haven't slept together in months. I think she knows I see other women."

"I don't doubt it, Mick. She's not stupid. Anyway, we are getting off the subject," said Tom impatiently. "Where is this leading? Get to the point. What is this scheme you have concocted to make money?"

"Come down here on Thursday night and we can discuss things properly," replied Mick. "You 've had a skinful already by the look of you. I want you stone-cold sober. I'm off and see if I can catch up with Norma."

Thursday couldn't come around quick enough for Tom. He kept going over and over what Mick had told him. Had Mick really found a way out of the mess they had both made of their lives? Tom speculated. *He has probably got a contract to work on a building site abroad. I could put Cathie and Phil in charge of the garage. I could do with a break and I could send my earnings home to pay the bills. Jenny would be glad to see the back of Mick for a while, I'm sure.*

"I'm off out tonight," Tom informed Cathie that Thursday afternoon. "Going to see someone about a new contract." He didn't particularly want her to know he was meeting Mick. She would start asking questions, as she knew Tom didn't class Mick as a mate. As far as she knew he just tolerated him as a brother-in-law.

And so, the lies began.

How could I have been so blind? My only excuse is I was so relieved that money was coming in to keep the business afloat. I was so thankful for that. I didn't question any details as to how Tom was earning the money. By that time, I had learned how to balance the books so as not to alert the taxman of anything suspicious. I suppose I was as guilty as Tom in my own way, Cathie admitted to herself.

Chapter Seven

The next Thursday evening Tom and Mick sat down in a quiet corner of the Red Dragon and over a pint of beer. Mick revealed his plans to Tom.

"It's not all legit'," Mick began. Tom heard warning bells. "But nothing can go wrong and we can make some easy money."

"Go on," said Tom. "I 'm open to any suggestions at the moment. Things are bad."

"You sure I can trust you, Tom?" Mick looked Tom in the eye. "Don't you go blabbing any of this to that pretty wife of yours." Mick waited.

"Hundred per cent," Tom nodded. "At this present time, I stand to lose everything I have ever worked for."

Mick drew his chair closer and lowered his voice.

"Do you remember Norma?" He began. "The tart I brought in here a while ago," Tom recalled the attractive dark-haired girl. She was not Mick's usual brassy blonde type. He nodded. "Well," continued Mick. "I have been getting pally with her lately for a reason. She has got it into her head that I will leave Jenny and the kids for her but I'm not ready for all that yet. I need money to go with." Tom was getting impatient.

"I didn't come here to listen to your women problems Mick. Get on with it." Mick looked around to make sure he was not being overheard.

"Norma works in the village shop and post office about four

miles from here," he started to explain. "In Llan-y -Wern. You know it, Tom?" Tom nodded. "I shot her a line that if we had enough money to start up somewhere else, I would divorce Jenny and marry her. She believes every word I tell her. More fool her, but she is useful at the moment so I keep her sweet. She is quite willing to come on board with my plan. She has been watching the owner of the post office for a while now when he opens the safe, and she has worked out the combination." Tom could see where this was going and he was becoming uncomfortable with what he was hearing.

"I have never done anything like this before, Mick. It's too risky. I don't want anything to do with it. I thought you had some legitimate plan to get some money, like working abroad or something." Mick was insistent.

"There's no risk to this Tom. I have worked it all out. Norma knows what night the safe holds the most money. She even suggested the week before a bank holiday when the safe holds the maximum amount. She needn't even know you are involved. We'll be careful not to leave any fingerprints. She has told me where the alarm is and the cable can be cut from the outside and we can easily get in around the back of the shop. I'll make sure Norma has a good alibi on the night and we'll give her a cut of the money to make doubly sure she keeps quiet. No one will suspect she had anything to do with it. She has worked there for years. Job done and a couple of thousand each for a night's work. Can't be bad."

Tom hesitated. "Why do you need me, Mick?" he asked. "You could do this job on your own and keep all the money."

"We need a car Tom, simple as that. That's your department. Something no one will take much notice of. Change the number plates just in case we are spotted. But Norma's boss doesn't have a security camera or a guard dog. He lives in the adjoining house. It's a quiet village where nothing ever happens. The police station is at Llanmerthyg, the nearest town four miles away."

"Are you sure you can trust this Norma?" Tom inquired.

"Sure, as Hell will never freeze over. Hers in love with me, poor cow. She'll do anything I ask."

"Let me think it over," Tom told him. "Let's not meet in here next time. Meet me in town in the Bricklayers Arms next Monday at eight. No one knows us in there."

"Right'o," Mick agreed. "It's foolproof Tom, I promise. You could pay off a few debts with the money, eh?" They drank up and left the pub.

"Did you get anywhere with that contract Tom?" Cathie asked tentatively when she had made him a cup of tea. She never knew these days how Tom would react to her questioning. To her relief, he seemed to be in a good mood.

"He seems keen to use us," Tom replied. "Just got to meet him again on Monday night to finalize things." He hugged her. "Maybe things will turn around for us Cathie." She didn't press the matter any further by asking the details at that moment. He would tell her in his own time she reasoned to herself. He probably wanted to secure the contract before building up her hopes.

"Till Monday then," she smiled. "Fingers crossed."

At eight o clock on Monday Tom and Mick met as arranged. To

their relief no one in the pub recognized them and they made their way to an inconspicuous corner to discuss Mick's idea in more detail. Tom was still hesitant but he was leaning towards the plan because of all the debt he was in. It would be a solution to everything. Mick had no qualms whatsoever.

"It's a way out for both of us Tom."

"It's hardly a way out," Tom reminded him. "It will just give me breathing space and give you some money to put towards whatever you decide to do in the future."

"Well, at least we will be doing something about things and not sitting moaning about everything. What harm can it do Tom? The owner of the shop will be well insured and not out of pocket."

Mick was gradually wearing down Tom's resolve. Little by little Tom was beginning to think it was not a bad idea. It would stop Cathie worrying about the business and maybe their relationship would improve. He thought to himself that if he went out two or three times a week in the evenings telling Cathie he was working he could top up the weekly takings for a few months and the books would balance better. Tom looked at Mick and nodded.

"Yes, it does make good sense if we plan it properly. But where can I say the money came from? That is the problem, Mick. Cathie is bound to want to know where I am going to earn the extra cash. You can just stick yours in a tidy place somewhere safe. I have to be careful to filter it into the business." Mick was silent. They both sat deep in thought.

At last, Mick came up with a plan.

"You have already told Cathie you were trying to finalize a

contract. Tell her it's not exactly a contract. You have met this rich businessman in the pub. He seems a bit of a dodgy character so you don't ask too many questions. But he approached you and asked for a price to take him to Manchester airport two or three evenings a week, wait around for a couple of hours and then bring him back. You could use your own car, tell her. No questions asked. You could top up your takings that way. Not enough to raise any suspicion but enough to pay off a few outstanding bills until business picks up. I can get some petrol receipts for you. What do you say?" Tom thought this over for a while.

"Sounds OK to me," he answered at last. "Pity I have to pay bills with the money though. I'll never see any of it for the risk I am taking."

"Well Tom, remember why you have agreed to this. Otherwise, you stand to lose everything."

"Too true," sighed Tom. "What a bloody mess I have got myself into."

Over another pint, they set a time and a date for the planned robbery. It would have to be on a weekday night before the following Bank Holiday. The safe would be full as money to pay pensions and child benefit which was delivered by security van on a Monday afternoon. Norma had already given Mick the combination of the safe. They decided on the Thursday night of that week.

When the next auction came around Tom bought three cars including a black Ford Cortina. They were a common car and he thought no one would take much notice of it. He had found some suitable number plates at the scrap yard and changed the original ones. They were all set. As time grew closer to the week of the planned robbery Tom was really on edge. Cathie and the children kept out of his way. She understood that all the worry of the bills piling up had brought on his black moods. She didn't know then that he had more than bills to worry over.

When the planned Thursday night came around Tom told Cathie he had a run to the airport. Luckily there was no moon that night. It was quite cloudy. He was very nervous as he drove the Cortina to pick up Mick from the end of his lane then on to the back of the shop. Tom looked at his watch. It was two in the morning. His stomach was in knots and his hands were shaking.

"What if some insomniac has seen me driving around here?"

"Quiet you, idiot," snapped Mick. "Get a grip on yourself and just concentrate on what you are doing. Now come on and don't touch anything without your gloves on." Silently they crept around the back of the building and found the wire to the alarm system. Mick was carrying a pair of wire cutters and a jemmy and he deftly cut the alarm cable.

"Right," he let out his breath. "The first job is done. Now we can get in without disturbing anyone. Come on Tom, keep up." Mick stuck the jemmy into the side of the windowsill by one of the hinges and with a bit of pushing and shoving managed to loosen the hinges and soon enough they were inside the shop. They breathed a sigh of relief at the silence. They went straight to the safe and Mick quickly opened it with the combination numbers Norma had given him. Tom was still shaking. He felt like throwing up.

"Get a hold of yourself and keep this bag open," growled Mick. They hurriedly filled the sack, shut the safe up again, grabbed their tools and made their way back to the car, making sure no one was around. Everywhere was silent, they didn't see a soul. Tom started up the car and they sped out on to the back road out of the village. Mick was ecstatic.

"How easy was that Tom?" he laughed. "I have never had so much money in my hands at any one time. Pull into the lane at my place and we'll count it." In the shelter of the lane when they reached Mick's place, Tom pulled the car over. He had stopped shaking. They opened up the bag and counted the money and split it between them. Mick keeping a bit extra to keep Norma quiet. They couldn't believe how easy it had been.

When he dropped Mick off Tom drove to his garage and put the original number plates back on the Cortina and hid most of the money in a safe place. Then he drove his own car home. He felt happier than he had for a long while. *I can pay off a few bills now and Cathie can stop worrying for a while. But she must never find out where the money has come from.*

Chapter Eight

Several weeks had passed and the police had got no further clues as to who had robbed the post office. It was the first serious crime in the area for over ten years. They were sifting through everything but to no avail. Norma was interviewed by the police and true to her word played innocent of any involvement. The police did suspect that she may have given the combination of the safe to someone but they failed to prove anything. Eventually, the interest in the case diminished. Mick and Tom scanned the local papers with ever-increasing confidence that they had got away with the robbery.

Cathie was happy and relieved that things were becoming more positive with their marriage and the business. She put it all down to having the extra income from Tom taking the businessman up and down to the airport. Fingers crossed this arrangement would continue till they got on top of their bills. She now put aside all doubts about Tom's infidelity. He seemed to be working extra hard and not wasting his evenings down at the pub. He only went out twice a week in the evenings and she knew he was working, as the takings were healthier than they had been for a while. Life was good again at last. The children were more settled and doing well at school now she and Tom were not rowing all the time. One thing niggled at her. She didn't feel that Tom was sharing her happier mood. He was a bit withdrawn.

"Are you OK Tom?" she inquired one morning over breakfast.

"I'm fine Cathie, why?"

"You seem so distant at times. I would love to know where your thoughts are." Tom smiled.

"I'm just tired, Cathie. All the extra driving I suppose," he lied. "I'm off down the garage so I'll see you later."

"We are doing alright though aren't we Tom?" she persisted. "You need to relax more. All work, you know what people say. Makes for a dull boy." He smiled at her again, driving his guilty thoughts to the back of his mind.

"I'm off now Cathie," He needed to escape her questioning. "We have a couple of cars in from the auctions I need to check over." She bent over to kiss him.

"Love you, Tom," she said. "Love you more," he answered.

Tom was very worried. The stolen money was running out. He had to think of something quickly. The business was slow and no new contracts were forthcoming. He was beginning to panic again. What could he do?

Later that day as he was taking a family to the airport an idea formed in his mind. In a couple of weeks, he would be taking Mrs. Thomas, one of his regular clients, to the airport. She liked to be taken everywhere in Tom's car. She thought of him as her personal chauffeur and Tom didn't mind the airport trips. She paid well and always gave him a big tip. She was a rich widow in her sixties and she owned a villa in Spain and often went there for weeks at a time. Her husband had owned a haulage company and she owned a large house on the edge of town. She had told Tom once in conversation that her husband didn't trust banks and also, he hated the thought of the taxman getting hold of all his money. Her husband had passed away twelve months ago and she loved to chat about him to Tom.

As he was driving along, Tom recalled this conversation. *I bet she has a mint of money stashed away in that house.* No one could see the house from the road.

As Tom's share of the money dwindled to a dangerously low level, he decided, out of desperation, to get in touch with Mick again. After all, they had got away with it once. Why not try it just one more time? They had been cautious and had not contacted one another since the robbery. He knew where to find Mick.

"Hi, how're things?" enquired Mick as Tom ordered a pint.

"They have been much better lately," admitted Tom. "But I have a problem and you can guess what that is." Mick nodded.

"I can, but we knew that didn't we Tom?" Tom nodded. "I've got Norma with me. She is just chatting to one of her mates. Meet me in the Bull and Heifer on Wednesday and we can talk then."

"OK," agreed Tom. "I hate having to do this."

"Won't be forever," answered Mick. "See you Wednesday."

On the Wednesday evening, Tom told Cathie he was popping out for a bit of business. She had learnt not to question his whereabouts. She told herself she just had to trust him. Tom found Mick sitting in the corner of the Bull and Heifer and joined him with a pint.

"How's Cathie and the kids," Mick began.

"They are fine," answered Tom. "Thinking they have a wonderful husband and father who works hard and keeps them safe. If only they knew the truth."

"Don't think that way," Mick told him sharply. "What we did

was easy money and we need it more than the government does at the moment. It's not as if we don't work hard and if those useless idiots in Parliament had handled things better and not put us in a recession, we would not be in this situation, so they owe us that money, don't they? My life is not all that rosy at the moment either and it's getting worse all the time. That bitch of a wife of mine is driving me mad. She has found out all about Norma. You can't keep a secret around here. She hates me with a vengeance and does as little as she possibly can for me. I'm lucky if she cooks a meal for me anymore. I think she would poison me if she thought she could get away with it. She's taken herself off into the spare room at night. But I can't get rid of Norma. She may spill the beans on us. You know, a scorned woman. Unpredictable. Women eh, trapped by one and now seem to be trapped again. I should have been a monk." Tom laughed.

"You, a monk. The nuns would have to watch out. You can't keep it in your pants."

"I suppose you are right Tom," Mick grinned. "But that's enough about my problems. I have one or two ideas floating round in my head. How about you?"

Mick told him he had been eyeing up one or two petrol stations out of the area. Tom was not keen.

"That would mean we would have to threaten an attendant."

"Yes," agreed Mick. "But we are not playing at this. It will be big money and it may take only one hit. We could stop then." Tom listened to his argument but was not convinced.

"I'm not a born criminal Mick. I hate having to do this."

"No one is a born criminal," Mick answered. "It's how life

deals the cards. Be a man and do what you have to do for your family."

"I have another idea," said Tom and he told Mick about his rich widowed client. "We wouldn't have to threaten anyone. No one would get hurt, Mick. What do you think? I am convinced she has stacks of money somewhere in the house. She is always popping over to Spain and from what she has let slip in conversation, she doesn't use a bank. It's worth a chance, don't you think?" Mick thought about it.

"Well, if she's away and lives on her own and no one can see the house from the road, I suppose it's worth having a look around." Tom felt relieved that Mick had not put up any objections. If he was forced to do a robbery it was better if no one was threatened. This woman had a big house and a villa in Spain. She would not miss a few thousand pounds, if she had that amount in the house. He was convinced she had, and it would be her own fault if it was stolen. Her husband should have put it in the bank for safety and paid his taxes like everyone else had to.

Mick stirred him out of his thoughts.

"OK, we'll give it a go. I only hope you are right about her keeping a stash in the house."

"She practically admitted it to me ages ago on one of our runs to the airport," said Tom.

Over another pint, they got down to business and discussed their plans. Once again Tom was to get a car from the auctions and change its number plate.

"We better not see each other again till I know the date for sure," advised Tom. "Can't be too careful. I'll be in touch soon."

Okay," replied Mick.

The following week, Tom was on his way to the airport with Mrs. Thomas. She was in a very chatty mood and looking forward to her holiday in Spain.

"It's too cold for my old bones over here Tom," she told him. "I am going for three months this time. Get most of this winter over with. My nephew will pop over here and there to keep the house aired and keep my pipes from freezing up." Tom's ears pricked up.

"I didn't know you had a nephew, Mrs. Thomas," he said, making conversation.

"Oh yes, Tom. He does odd jobs for me here and there. I have told him I am leaving my money to him in my will so he is very obliging."

"That's very cynical of you," laughed Tom. "Does he stay over?" he inquired casually.

"Oh no," replied Mrs. Thomas. "He only lives about twenty miles away. He has a wife and family," Tom thought to himself. *Thank goodness for that It would have scuppered our plans good and proper if he had lived next door or stayed in the house while she was away.*

The next evening, he popped into the Red Dragon to find Mick. As usual Mick was propping up the bar chatting to Norma.

"Jenny is over at our house and she sent me over to give you a message," he said loudly to get Mick's attention. Norma rolled her eyes as Mick cursed and went over to speak to Tom.

"We're on for tomorrow night," Tom spoke quietly. "Bring

the jemmy. I'll pick you up on your lane about midnight." Mick nodded.

"Tell that bitch I'll get back when I feel like it," Mick said loudly within earshot of Norma. "Bloody cheek. Thinks she owns me. Give us another pint Emerys and a Bacardi and coke for Norma." Tom had disappeared when he turned around.

Tom had informed Cathie that he would be out the next night on an airport run. He had acquired a car and changed the number plates as before. He picked up the car from the garage and set off to meet Mick. With his dark coat on, walking down the narrow lane, Tom nearly ran over Mick.

"Bloody hell Tom, you nearly 'ad me there."

"Get in and shut up. I missed you, didn't I? It's pitch black in this lane." As they carried on towards Mrs. Thomas' place Tom filled Mick in on some of the details.

"We'll leave the car well away from the house and go over the backfields. No one will see us. I've been in the house. The French windows are not very secure. Should be a doddle getting in." Tom drove up a lane across the field from the house.

"No one lives up here. I've checked," he told Mick. "If anyone did happen to be passing which is highly unlikely at this time of night, they would probably think it was only a courting couple parked up."

They made their way over the field. They had come prepared and both of them wore old shoes that they planned to ditch after the robbery in case the police examined the footprints. They checked no one was around. All was silent except for the odd owl hooting. It was a cloudy night.

"Black as coal out 'ere thank the Lord," whispered Mick. "Just the job." Tom had already checked for an alarm system or a guard dog on the premises when he had picked up Mrs. Thomas. She had neither. Apparently, she had lived in the house for twenty years and never had any trouble with burglars.

As they approached the house they put on their gloves. Mick set about forcing the lock on the French windows, and very soon they were inside the house. They breathed a sigh of relief.

"Now where would anyone hide cash? Hope to God it's not in a safe," said Mick.

"Well, she's never bothered about security very much so I doubt it," reasoned Tom. "Come on, you start down here and I'll go upstairs." They started rummaging through the drawers and cupboards in the house and after an hour had found nothing. Tom had found jewellery in one of the bedrooms but they didn't want that as it would be difficult to get rid of. That would be a last resort.

"You've brought me on a bloody wild goose chase," Mick snarled at Tom and grabbed him around the throat. "I should never have listened to your hair-brained ideas." He gave Tom a shove.

"Take it easy Mick," Tom was shocked that his brother-in-law had threatened him and tried to calm him down. "Losing your temper with me won't get you anywhere. Calm down and let's think. Now, where would an old lady keep the money? She wasn't bothered about security so I reckon it's in her bedroom somewhere. I'm going to have another look."

"I'll go over the study again but God 'elp you if we don't find it," grumbled Mick.

Tom was convinced the money was in the house and made his way towards Mrs. Thomas' bedroom again. He sat down on the bed to think.

It must be in here somewhere. He had checked the dressing table and under the mattress and in the wardrobe. Nothing. They had already checked behind the pictures for a safe. Tom reasoned that the only place must be behind a false wall if it was here at all. Carefully he checked the walls and the back of the wardrobe. As he moved some shoes to check the back of the wardrobe, he lifted up the piece of carpet the shoes were on. On the wardrobe base, he noticed a small hole in it to fit a finger. Hands shaking, he lifted up the wooden base.

"It's here Mick, I've found it," he shouted excitedly. Mick rushed up the stairs two at a time.

Tom was staring at two tin boxes in the space underneath the floor of the wardrobe.

"Get them out then and open them up. Move over, I'll do it." Mick shoved Tom aside, leaned in and lifted out the boxes. They were not locked and he hastily opened them.

"Bloody 'ell Mick," Tom sounded relieved. "There must be nigh on four grand in these boxes. Crafty cow. Her husband must have stashed it away to avoid the taxman." Mick was less enthusiastic.

"Not that much for a night's work," he grumbled, "Hardly worth the bloody trouble."

"You ungrateful bugger Mick. It's twice as much as what we got from the post office and there was no risk. A much better idea than yours. No one was threatened. You are getting too greedy. Come on, let's empty the boxes and put them back. It will be months before she discovers it has gone. I doubt if her nephew knows she keeps money hidden in here. We can close the French windows again. The nephew probably won't examine them closely as he won't suspect anything. Why would he? It's foolproof."

"OK let's get out of here," grumbled Mick. "This is not going to set me up for life is it?" he muttered. Tom did not answer.

It will keep me going for a while though and hopefully keep the business from going under, Tom thought to himself.

Chapter Nine

Mick's mood had not lifted by the time Tom dropped him off in his lane. It was months later before Jenny opened up to Cathie about what had gone on that night.

Jenny was in the kitchen making herself a cup of tea when Mick walked in. He startled her. She had not heard his van pull up.

"Thought you were out for the night," she said. Mick was just as surprised to find her up in the middle of the night.

"What are you doing up?" She could sense he was in a foul mood.

"I couldn't sleep. It may not have crossed your mind but I do wonder if you have turned the van over and are lying in a ditch somewhere. But most of the time I think you are in the back of your van having it off with that tart of yours." As soon as she had said that she knew she had pushed him too far but she couldn't stop herself. With that remark, Mick hit Jenny across the face with full force. She staggered backwards, reeling across the kitchen.

"At least she's all woman, not an excuse for one like you. You've never known how to treat a man."

"She's welcome to you," answered Jenny rubbing her face. "Does she know you beat up women? I'll have to tell her. She may not think you are much of a man after all." Mick could not hold back his temper. He grabbed Jenny and punched her in the stomach. Winded, she dropped to the floor and he kicked her hard. She curled up in a ball and put her hands over her head to instinctively protect herself. He had done this many times before and she knew that if she lay still, he would stop.

"I hate you with a vengeance, you bitch. You trapped me into marrying you." He put his head in his hands. Jenny stayed still in case he started again. Mick glanced at her in contempt and made his way up to bed.

Gradually Jenny dragged herself on to a chair. She was sobbing quietly and rocking to and fro. She would have to tell the girls in the morning that she had fallen over outside. She felt too ashamed and humiliated to admit to anyone that she had taken a beating. She lay on the sofa to gather her thoughts and her strength together. She vowed then to herself that she would get her revenge when the opportunity arose. She was determined to get out of her situation and not spend the rest of her life covering up and pretending she had a good solid marriage. She had read about women who did that and in the end they either ended up dead or without any self-esteem left.

Oh no, that was not going to happen. She was angry now. She envisaged cutting the brake cables on his van or maybe poisoning him so he would die in agony. Maybe ground glass in his dinner. He was no father to her girls. They wouldn't miss him.

With these thoughts fixed in her mind, she gathered up some strength and slowly made her way upstairs to get washed and dressed. Mick would soon have to be up and out of the house to go to work and when the children had got off to school, she could have a long soak in the bath.

She made up her mind not to tell Cathie. She had never told her any of it. She couldn't bear the humiliation and also, she didn't want Tom stirring up trouble. Mick would only beat her up again if he found out she had been blabbing to Cathie and Tom. Best just let things settle and try to keep out of Mick's way as much as possible at the moment. She did wonder to herself what had put him in such a bad mood. Maybe he had not been getting on with the tart. She hoped in a way that was not the case. The more he stayed away the better Jenny liked it. There was nothing left of their marriage now.

Tom cuddled up to Cathie when he got into bed. She put her arm around him sleepily and he looked across at her.

"I am so sorry for everything," he whispered. She didn't hear him. "I only want to make things right for you and the kids. I am not a greedy person." He couldn't get off to sleep. His conscience was bothering him too much. They had robbed a vulnerable old lady. *What would his Army pals think of him now if they knew? Just too big headed. Wouldn't listen. Wanted to run before he could walk.* He chastised himself mentally. *Well, that's the last time, for definite. No matter what Mick says. He is becoming far too greedy. I didn't like the way he turned on me tonight. I will top up the takings each week with my cut and hope we can get straight soon.* He lay there tossing and turning and staring at the ceiling until six o clock, then went downstairs and made a cup of tea. He had not shut his eyes all night.

"Didn't hear you come in last night. Did it go ok? Cathie was busy getting the children ready for school. "Eat your cereal, Neil. It's a long time until dinner. Have any of you got P.E. today? Your kits are washed and pressed. Hurry up and Dad will give you a lift to school." They scurried about and Tom and Cathie had no time to chat. For that he was relieved. He hated telling lies.

He had changed the number plates back and checked the car over before telling Phil to put it through an M.O.T. And they would put it in the auction again.

"We can make a profit on it once it's got a certificate," he reasoned.

"If you say so," answered Phil. "Hardly worth the trouble was it? We need to pick up an old classic or two and do them up. Something we can really make a profit on. There's money in classic cars."

"You are absolutely right, Phil." he agreed. "We will keep an eye out. Money is not as tight as it was. We can afford to speculate a bit."

"That is good news, Tom, said Phil. "It's been a bit of a struggle, hasn't it?"

"I think I'll take the wife out for a nice meal tonight," said Tom. "I'll just pop over and tell Cathie to arrange a babysitter."

Cathie was filling in for Megan that afternoon when Tom caught up with her.

"Hiya gorgeous, how about a date tonight?" Tom called to her.

"Well, you are in a good mood, Tom. Have you won on the horses?"

"I wish," Tom answered laughing. "No, things are getting better and I remember you telling me not to be such a dull boy. We'll have a nice meal and a bottle of wine if you can get someone to look after the kids."

"Not a problem," said Cathie. "I'll go home a bit earlier and put on my best frock. It's ages since we went out together."

Chapter Ten

Mick was not a happy man. Jenny and the children kept out of his way as much as possible. They ate before he came in from work. His dinner was either non-existent or shriveled up in the oven. These days he usually got washed and changed when he had finished work and headed for the chip shop.

"What a miserable existence," he was talking to himself as he drove to work one morning. "A miserable so-called wife who does absolutely nothing for me and a fancy piece who wants money spent on her and is always nagging at me to get a divorce. I'll stop that bitch's housekeeping, that's what I'll do if she carries on. The only thing she cares about is that damned smallholding and the kids. If I stopped paying the bills, she would have to toe the line 'till it suited me otherwise. Yes, that' s what I'll do," Mick resolved.

That evening when he came in, he marched in and stood over Jenny.

"I want to talk to you." Her stomach was in knots these days when she heard his van pull up but she would never show that she was afraid of him.

"About what?" she inquired carrying on with preparing the dinner. "I've got nothing to say to you."

Through gritted teeth he explained slowly exactly what would happen.

"If you don't cook me decent meals and stop serving me dried up shit, I will stop your housekeeping. And if I don't get my washing and ironing done every week, I will not pay the rent.

I'm nobody's fool. Do you understand?"

She was backed into a corner. She sold her eggs and some produce down the market once a week but it was not enough to keep her and the kids. She did not want to lose her home. She would be able to take a job soon and then she would be able to manage but the children were not quite old enough yet. For some time, she had been planning her future for when she did finally rid herself of her cheating, violent husband one way or another.

"Well, I haven't got much of a choice then have I," she snapped back at him. "But you will never be certain I haven't put something in your dinner," she threatened. "And if you ever lay a finger on me again, I will have you banged up and no mistake." He laughed.

"Just you make sure I have decent meal and clean clothes to wear in future, or else. I'm sick already of looking at your ugly mug, I'm off out." He slammed the door and drove off down the lane.

Jenny breathed a sigh of relief. She was shaking inwardly but proud of herself for standing up to him. She could relax for the evening now.

"Come on down, girls. Dad has gone out. Tea is ready." Later that evening she thought over what Mick had said.

I will be able to get rid of him soon if he doesn't go first. I have got plenty of witnesses as to his carryings on with that tart, Norma. When I divorce him, he will have to pay maintenance for the girls. I can earn the rest. We will be able to stay here in peace without the fear of him turning up. Things will have to get better soon.

Mick headed for the Red Dragon to cool his temper. He needed some breathing space. He was even more determined than ever to change his life. He didn't want to be one of those men he talked to down at the pub, who grew old, full of regrets for what might have been.

"You're quiet tonight," remarked Emrys, the landlord.

"Got a lot on my mind," growled Mick. Emrys moved on to his next customer. As a landlord, he knew when to make conversation and when to leave well alone, but he couldn't help thinking to himself,

Two women on the go, it's impossible to keep both of them happy. No wonder he is so miserable. One woman is enough of a handful for any man.

Tom and Mick had agreed not to contact each other for four weeks. Tom was busy at the garage and he wouldn't care if he didn't see Mick for even longer. He was hoping this last extra boost of stolen money would put his business back on its feet. He and Cathie were very happy at the moment, free of money worries for the time being.

Mick brooded over his pint. Thoughts were churning around in his head.

I have promised Norma that I'll get a divorce and take her to Australia. Now she wants to start a family. She will have to ditch that idea if she wants to stay with me. I don't even know if I want her tagging along anyway. I can make a good life for myself as a trucker. No life for a woman. But what if she opens her trap about the post office robbery if I give her the elbow? She could do that with an anonymous phone call. What a mess. He sighed.

"Stick another pint in there Emrys, will you."

Mick joined in with the darts team. Anything to take his mind off his troubles. It passed an evening and about ten-thirty he finished his drink and made his way home along the back road, hoping he didn't meet a copper and get done for driving over the limit.

Chapter Eleven

Over the next few weeks, Mick spent his evenings, when he was not seeing Norma, cruising around, locating several petrol stations and studying when their quiet periods were. He still had that idea in his head for making some quick money He did not have the money he wanted to start his new life. He made a mental note of which petrol stations opened late or all night and tried to check out their security systems. He thought Tom's idea of robbing houses when he knew they were on holiday was a bit too hit and miss. He needed to know the risk would be worth it. He needed enough money for his passage to Australia and to buy a truck and maybe to buy a place to live if he decided to take Norma. These plans were constantly in his head and he was determined to get what he wanted.

When the four weeks were finally up, he called in at Tom's garage.

"Come down the pub later," he called to Tom. "I want to talk to you." Tom was reluctant to go. He knew what Mick wanted. Things were going well for Tom at the moment and he didn't want to risk any more robberies. He had not heard that Mrs. Thomas' nephew had come across anything suspicious. There was nothing in any of the local papers. The only worry would be when Mrs. Thomas next decided to check her boxes. By then the police would have no idea when she had been robbed. Tom had a feeling she might not even report it. It could open a can of worms as to why she had so much money hidden in the house.

"I'm busy all this week, Mick," Tom replied. "Can we make

it some other time?"

"No, we bloody well can't," Mick snapped back. He lowered his voice. "You are in this as much as me. Just be there or else." Tom was taken aback once again at this threatening behaviour. He didn't want Mick making a scene in the garage so he agreed to meet him that evening.

Over a pint, Mick seemed a lot calmer. He asked after Cathie and the kids and if the business was doing well. Tom filled him in on all his questions and Mick smiled. Mick didn't usually smile and Tom sensed it was a forced effort.

"How're things with you?" Tom inquired.

"Don't ask. I'm as miserable as sin these days. I go from one woman who never speaks to me to one who never shuts up nagging me to get a divorce."

"If I were in your shoes, Mick, I would just pack a bag and bugger off somewhere away from here."

"It has crossed my mind, Tom. But it is too risky. Jenny would have the social on me for maintenance and Norma might let the police know we had done the robbery. It only takes an anonymous phone call. I wouldn't trust her if I dumped her."

"Fair point," Tom agreed.

"Listen, Tom, I have been thinking," Mick said quietly. Tom groaned to himself. "Can we go back to my original idea of doing over a petrol station? I have been checking out a few and there is one in particular on the express-way, all on its own and only one kiosk attendant on at night. Wouldn't be too risky." Tom took a deep breath.

"I'm not doing it, Mick. Absolutely not. I'm OK for money

at the moment. It's too risky. We could go away for years if we were caught." Mick was stumped. He had known it would be hard to persuade Tom to come in on this one. Tom wasn't so desperate for money as he was. He would have to change his tactics. He decided to approach Cathie.

"Hello Mick, long time no see," said Cathie, surprised to see her brother-in-law. It had been months since she had seen him and she liked it that way. "How's Jenny and the kids? What with me working at the garage and her working at your place we hardly ever get time for a catch up these days. Tell her we must get together soon and I will ring her."

"Jenny is fine," answered Mick. "Busy as ever. She has a market stall two days a week now. Kids are doing well at school. Growing up fast, like yours." Cathie had done with pleasantries. It was always an effort to be pleasant to her brother-in-law.

"What brings you here Mick?" she inquired.

"Is Tom around? I need to see him about some work on the van." Mick knew Tom was not around. He had seen him drive off in the minibus.

"Sorry, Mick. You have just missed him. He has gone off on a school run. He'll be about half an hour."

"It's good that you are kept busy anyway," replied Mick. "Sorry to hear he has lost the night runs to the airport." Cathie was puzzled.

"What do you mean, Mick. He hasn't lost the contract as far as I know. You must be mistaken. Tom still does the airport run on a Tuesday and a Thursday night."

"Well, he was sitting in the Mason's Arms last Thursday night. I called in on my way home for some cigarettes. I was surprised to see him. I may be speaking out of turn here Cathie. I thought you knew. I shouldn't have opened my big mouth."

"No, go on Mick. If you know something I don't then I want to hear it. I don't understand though. He brings in the money from the runs. Are you sure it was Tom that you saw?"

"I spoke to him, Cathie. He was with that woman who works for you. What's her name? Megan? They seemed pretty cosy together now I come to think of it." Cathie felt as if someone had punched her in the stomach. She went very pale. Mick watched her reaction and thought to himself,

That's done it. You will play it my way from now on, Tom, my old son. Cathie tried to defend Tom.

"You must be mistaken, Mick. Tom would never lie or cheat on me. We are getting along really well at the moment. I'll talk to him when he gets back. I'm sure there's a valid explanation."

"Ok Cathie, I'm sure there is. Sorry if I've spoken out of turn. I'll call around the garage tomorrow to see about an estimate for the van. I'll give Jenny your message. Bye then."

Cathie couldn't concentrate. She couldn't wait for her shift to end. Megan would be taking over from her. They had never been friends. Cathie had always suspected that Megan fancied Tom. She barely spoke to her as she gave her an update on the bookings and handed over the keys.

When Tom came in that evening for his tea, he felt the atmosphere straight away.

"What's up, darling," he asked. "Have I done something

wrong?"

"I'll talk to you when the kids are in bed," was all he could get out of her.

When the children were all settled in their rooms, she turned on Tom.

"How could you tell me such a pack of lies?" she began. Tom was racking his brains as to what she was referring, so he let her carry on. "Are you seeing that Megan? She is married and may I remind you, so are you. Why Tom? What are you doing? Do you want this family to split up for the sake of that little tramp? I thought we were happy." She was crying with temper. Tom was relieved that she had not found out anything else. He grabbed her arm.

"Where has all this come from?" He was genuinely surprised. "I'm not interested in Megan. She is just an employee. Honest Cathie. Why would I choose her over you and risk losing you and the kids? Come on." She sat down and took a breath.

"Mick was round here earlier. He didn't mean to say anything but he let it slip that you no longer have the contracts for the airport on a Tuesday and Thursday nights. He said he saw you in the pub last Thursday, the Mason's Arms, and you were sitting with that Megan." She looked at Tom for a denial.

The devious bastard. I know what he's at. Tom knew he was backed into a corner and would have to come up with some sort of explanation.

"I'm sorry Cathie. No, we don't have the contract anymore. I didn't know how to tell you. It was a big boost to the takings. I went to the Masons Arms to have a quiet think. I was only chatting with Megan because she was in there. I had no intention of seeing her. You have to believe that. I would not lie. Please trust me."

"How can I trust you? If you lie about one thing you will lie about another." Tom was getting agitated and he cursed Mick under his breath.

"I did not tell you about the contract because I was hoping something else would come up. You are such a worry guts. And I swear on the kid's lives I am not having an affair. Is that convincing enough for you?" She wanted to believe him.

"If all you say is true, why is the money still coming in?"

"He was a week behind with the payments, Cathie. I knew I would have to tell you this week." She was beginning to believe him.

"What are we going to do now the takings are down Tom? The bills will start piling up again." Tom felt easier now Cathie had calmed down.

"We'll be all right love, I have a few irons in the fire down at the garage. I am sorry Mick gave you all this worry. I was going to tell you. He has a big mouth at times." Cathie nodded in agreement. She was relieved that Tom had come clean with her. He would think of another way to bring in the money. She had to have faith in him.

She loved him.

The next evening Tom told Cathie he was going to have it out with Mick for shouting his mouth off and causing trouble between them.

"I'll get a babysitter and we can both go if you like,"

suggested Cathie.

"No, I had better go on my own. It's not going to be a very social evening. I have a few choice words to say to him and it might get nasty. You know what a temper he has."

"All right," agreed Cathie reluctantly. "But do be careful. I don't know how my sister puts up with him but they seem to muddle along, which reminds me, I must give her a ring."

Chapter Twelve

Tom knew Mick would be down the pub that evening. It was one of his regular nights to see Norma. Megan was sitting at the bar as usual and he nodded to her.

"Come and sit over here Tom. I could do with the company," she called.

"Not just now," he answered. "I have a bit of business I want to discuss with Mick." The last thing he wanted at this time was to be seen chatting to Megan.

He beckoned Mick over and told him he wanted a private word. Mick feigned surprise.

"Won't be a mo," he called over to Norma. "I thought you had decided not to go ahead with my suggestion," Mick remarked.

"You know bloody well why I am here Mick. Blabbing your mouth off to Cathie. You knew mentioning Megan would stir up trouble and get me down here didn't you?" Tom was fuming. Mick laughed.

"There's plenty more where that came from Tom. I have witnesses that you have spent more than your fair share of evenings in the back of your car with that little employee of yours. Now if you want me to keep stum you will agree to my next little scheme. You can't just back out when it suits you. It doesn't work that way. We are in this together or have you forgotten?"

"I wish to God I had never got involved in all this. Much

easier to have let the business go with a clear conscience than have all this worry now."

"Easy to say that now Tom, isn't it?" Mick was being patronizing and Tom's fists were itching to smack him one, but that would lead to a whole new set of questions with the drinkers in the pub as to what had made Tom lose his temper.

He was cornered. He sat down and stared at Mick.

"What you are threatening is blackmail. I never thought you would stoop so low," he snarled at Mick.

"Them's harsh words, Tom. I'm just helping us both out. You'll thank me one day when you and that precious wife of yours are in the money. You'll see. Now I've got to get back to Norma. She'll be wondering what is so important. She'll guess we are planning something if we are not careful. Now, are you ready to listen to my plan? I'll meet you in the Bull and Heifer at the usual time on Thursday."

Tom sat mooning over his pint. He felt Megan was trying to catch his eye but he wasn't in the mood for company, least of all hers. He drank up and went home.

"I've had it out with Mick, Cathie. He did apologize. He's just jealous of our marriage. He and Jenny are at each other's throats all the time according to him. In his warped mind, he wanted to stir up trouble for us to make himself feel better. He's an odd sort. Best not take anything he says to heart. He's a bit twisted."

"It's forgotten already." Cathie smiled at Tom. "I'm mainly worried about drumming up more business for us to compensate for the loss of that contract." Tom gave her a hug.

"Leave it to me. Something will come along. No more worrying now."

Mick was sitting in the corner of the Bull and Heifer when Tom walked in. He bought himself a pint and sat down opposite Mick.

"That was a nasty stunt you pulled," he began. "You have given me no choice but to go along with your plans. I think you're an evil bastard. I must have been desperate to get mixed up in all this."

"As I recall, you were desperate," answered Mick. "You bit my hand off to help you out of trouble a few months ago. Now, I am sure Cathie would be all ears to find out a bit more about your secret little liaison with Megan."

"That was ages ago and you know it," answered Tom glaring across the table. "You know it is all over, she has had a couple more men since then."

"That may be so Tom," said Mick in a patronizing tone, "but you did have an affair. You can't deny it. She still fancies you as well you know. You've only to give her an ounce of encouragement and she would drop the bloke she is with like a stone. She keeps quiet about the past as she wants to keep her job and I think she is still hoping for a chance with you. Divorce could be on the cards for you if the truth came out. You would lose everything." He stared at Tom then went to the bar for another pint.

When he sat down again Tom lowered his voice. "You are a real nasty bugger Mick when you want your own way. I never thought you would resort to blackmailing tactics. We are supposed to be family."

"You've only seen one side of me, Tom. Now I'm afraid you have seen the other. I always get my own way. Now we both know where we stand. Let's get down to business."

Mick told Tom the exact petrol station he had pinpointed to be the easiest to raid. It was about fifteen miles away on the expressway. It was in an isolated spot and opened for twenty-four hours. There was only one attendant on at night who manned the kiosk.

"I've watched it a few times," Mick continued." And about two in the morning is about the best time to hit it."

"There must be security," questioned Tom.

"Well, from what I can see there is no guard dog. There is probably a button somewhere under the counter linked to the police station and that is five miles away. We have to chance there is no patrol car in the area."

"Seems pretty daft to me that there isn't much in the way of security," said Tom. "These country places are asking for trouble."

Mick was glad Tom had resigned himself to take part in the robbery. He needed Tom to supply a car and now he had a hold over Tom he knew he could rely on him a hundred per cent. He carried on.

"I have clocked when they change shifts. It's at ten o' clock, so by two in the morning the night attendant will be either sleeping or eating his supper. There is hardly any traffic about at that time of the morning. We will be on him before he knows what's hit him. He won't have time to press any alarm buttons.

Like the last time, we can leave the car around the back and get in through the window at the back. I forgot to mention this to you. On the day we decide on, I will fill the truck up with petrol, use the toilet and unlatch the window at the back. I will make sure no one sees me. They will never notice the window has been unlocked. No one checks."

"How do you know that," questioned Tom. "There are two things we could have a problem with. The window may be closed or there could be a police patrol car in the area." Mick was getting wound up again and raised his voice.

"Don't be so defeatist for God's sake."

"Keep your voice down Mick, will you," The last thing Tom wanted was Mick causing attention to them.

"There is bound to be a risk, Tom," Mick was in control of himself again. "But it is small and if we are not sure of anything we can pull out. I promise you that. I don't want to end up in Nick. Agreed?"

"I suppose so," Tom answered begrudgingly.

"Now, being as its winter and cold at night, that can work to our advantage," Mick began again. We can wear a balaclava and a scarf over our faces and no one will think it odd. We can wear heavy overcoats and it will be difficult for the attendant to give the police a good description of us, don't you think? I can burn the coats and shoes and stuff when Jenny is at the market.

"But what if anyone is around and sees us in the car?" Tom was very unsure of the plan. Mick gave an exasperated sigh.

"We've covered all that from the last job. To repeat myself, you buy one at the auction, get some false plates, the next day tell Phil you want it MOT'd and resprayed as you want a quick profit and put it into a different auction the following week. Smart eh?"

"I hope you are right and no one comes sniffing around the garage asking questions or Phil may say something he shouldn't," muttered Tom.

Tom was turning all the information over in his mind.

"And how do we get the money once we are in the building," enquired Tom.

"You leave all that to me Tom, I'll handle the attendant. Just you keep an eye out for another car pulling in for petrol or the police doing routine patrol. When I 'm busy in the office you put the 'closed sign' up on the forecourt and hopefully anyone around will drive off. I've driven past at two in the morning on four separate occasions and have never seen any cars around. This one will be worth it Tom. We won't have to do it again and we'll both be set up for life."

Tom was in a no-win situation. He could see no way out. He hated the thought of going through all this again but he hated, even more, the fact that Mick would have no qualms about resorting to blackmail. He had the knowledge to ruin his marriage. He was beginning to hate Mick and he wished to goodness he had trusted his initial instincts about his brother-in-law and kept well away from him.

'Too late now. I only hope he stops at this one and he and Norma disappear down-under. The business should be back on its feet soon. The recession can't last forever.

Chapter Thirteen

They kept an eye on the weather and chose a particularly dark, cloudy Friday night. There was no moon. Tom had checked the car over. They had hidden the clothes and shoes they would wear for the robbery in the boot of the car. Tom had to lie to Cathie again as he made up an excuse to go out for the evening. He told her he had bumped into Mrs. Evans the previous morning and she had asked him to run her and her sister to Birmingham airport on the Friday evening. "Sorry I didn't put it in the diary, Cathie. It slipped my mind and I very nearly forgot about the booking." He put on his apologetic face.

Lies slip out of my mouth so easily. I could tell her anything and she wouldn't doubt me. I'm such a rotten pig to have to do this to her.

"That's ok Tom." Cathie smiled at him. "Good that we have the work. I'll put my feet up and watch a girlie film when the kids are in bed. You drive carefully now. I expect I will be asleep when you come in. Give Mrs. Evans my regards. She is lucky to have the money not to have to rely on public transport. I hope she gives you a good tip." Tom hugged his children and kissed Cathie and hurried out of the door before he had to think up any more lies.

He drove to the garage. His stomach was in knots. The garage was locked and in darkness. Megan and Phil had gone home a while ago. He started the engine on the car he and Mick planned to use. He locked his own car in the garage and set off to pick up Mick from his lane.

"God, it's brass-monkey weather tonight all right," Mick remarked to Tom as he jumped into the car. "We'll need those scarves and overcoats."

"I wish it was all over," grumbled Tom. "I've had to tell Cathie so many lies. I hope our luck holds out."

"You are a worry guts, Tom. You'd never make a living as a gangster that's for sure," grinned Mick. "Put the hammer down and let's get there. I can't wait to get my hands on all that lolly."

Tom put his foot down and they sped along the back lanes. They met no traffic. They joined the expressway about a mile from the garage and only passed a couple of cars going in the opposite direction. They parked up around the back of the garage as planned. Mick gathered up a bag to take with him into the garage.

"Well, here goes," said Mick. "You keep your eyes peeled and be ready to drive off when I come out," he instructed Tom.

"Will do, and good luck," replied Tom.

Tom reflected on the situation years later. At that particular moment, he would have had the opportunity to ditch Mick there and then and drive off while Mick was in the process of threatening the attendant. Why didn't he think of that at the time instead of blindly following Mick into deeper waters? He could have turned on Mick just as Mick had no qualms in blackmailing him. But Tom's brain didn't work like that. He was committed to the plan and had to stand by it. Maybe his Army training had bred such obligation.

Mick crept up to the back window of the garage, keeping well into the shadows. He stopped and listened as he heard voices.

"Thank the Lord for that," he whispered to himself. "It's a radio playing. He won't hear me coming with that on." The window catch was as he had left it earlier in the day and he easily slid inside. He adjusted his eyes to the dim light and looked around to get his bearings. A crack of light shone under the office door. Mick took a baseball bat out of his bag and slowly opened the office door. The door squeaked and the attendant shot off his chair.

"God Almighty, where did you come from," he shouted.

"Just shut up and keep your hands on the counter," snarled Mick wielding the bat. The attendant paled and did as Mick had instructed. "Now where's the money?"

The attendant glanced towards the till.

"I mean the takings you idiot," shouted Mick. "Open the safe," he growled. The attendant began to tremble.

"I can't," he stammered an explanation. "The manager opens it each morning when the security van pulls up. He puts the days' takings in the safe before he goes home. I can only open the till." Mick raised the baseball bat. He was losing his temper and the attendant cowered in terror.

"You're lying," Mick shouted. "Open the bloody safe." As he raised the bat ready to strike, the attendant put his hands over his head to protect himself. Just at that moment, Mick heard Tom shouting from the back window.

"Get a move on for God's sake. There's a patrol car just gone past. They may come back." Mick threw the bat on the floor in frustration.

"I am telling you the truth," the attendant was shaking and almost in tears. "This job is not worth having my head caved in for." Mick realized he had made a serious error in taking for granted that a night attendant would have the keys to the safe. What a fool. Well, they wouldn't go away empty-handed.

"Get that till open," he snarled again at the attendant. There were only a few notes in the till.

"There's no bloody money in here," shouted Mick as he snatched what was in the till, and began to empty the shelves of cigarettes.

"You, get into the toilet," he pushed the attendant in and barricaded the door. "You can stay there 'till the morning." Mick picked up the baseball bat and the bag and ran to the car. "Let's get out of here. What a bloody waste of time that was."

Tom looked over at him as they drove away.

"Don't tell me you didn't get anything. And you had a weapon as well. You kept quiet about the baseball bat. What possessed you? We'll get years if we are caught with a weapon. What the hell went wrong?" Mick didn't answer for a while. Finally, he explained.

"The guy opened the safe but he did tell me the money had been banked that afternoon as the manager had to go to a funeral in the morning and wouldn't be there to hand it over to the security van. It's not my bloody fault someone died and they changed the routine." He was lying through his back teeth to save face.

"I filled the sack with cigarettes. We'll flog those. It wasn't a complete disaster."

"We've risked years in the nick for a few smokes. Nice one Mick," replied Tom sarcastically. They drove the rest of the way in silence.

The robbery made the headlines in the local paper. There was never much local news so they gave it a big spread. Maldwyn Williams, the attendant had been found the next morning by a customer who had gone to pay for his petrol and had heard the hammering and the shouting. The customer was as shocked as Maldwyn, who quickly informed the police over what had happened. The police examined the window where the thief had got in and they surmised that one of the staff must have carelessly left it open They questioned Maldwyn intensely as to why he had not done his job properly and made sure all windows were locked. There were no fingerprints and the police concluded that the robbers must have been watching the petrol station for some time and this was well planned. But, on their report they concluded it was not an inside job, as staff would know who held the keys and when the money was banked. This robbery was done by amateurs.

Maldwyn couldn't describe the robber as his face was well hidden with a balaclava and a scarf and he had been too frightened to take in much detail. He told the police he had no idea where the robber had appeared from. No vehicle had pulled on to the forecourt.

"Probably asleep, were you?" asked the inspector.

"Well maybe," answered Maldwyn. "It's a long old night and I'm not paid to be on guard for break-ins."

"Fair comment. Maybe you should ask your manager for a guard dog. It would be company for you and I don't expect we'd have been called to your garage if they knew there was a dog around. You could have been killed out here on your own." Maldwyn shook his head.

"This has been a real eye-opener for me. I have given in my

notice. It's not worth risking my life for the pittance I get paid. They can stick their job."

The police interviewed all the staff and failed to get any leads. They didn't have one clue to lead them to the robbers.

The next day Tom sprayed the car they had used. He had already checked it over mechanically and the next evening he and Phil drove to the auctions.

"We should get a good price for this one Tom," Phil remarked. "You have done a good spray job on her. She looks like new."

"Hope so Phil, fingers crossed. We need a bit of cash at the moment. I have my eye on a classic to renovate. That's our next project."

"Sounds interesting," answered Phil. "I'm glad business is picking up for us Tom. We 'll be millionaires yet."

Mick was in a thoroughly bad mood. The garage robbery had ended up a complete disaster. He had high hopes of raking in a stash of money, enough to set him up for his new life. Instead, he could only add the meagre amount to the sum he had already saved. It was nowhere near enough. He was beginning to think like Tom and to set his sights lower. He may have to give up his dream of a new life in Australia. He may have to aim for somewhere nearer. France, maybe. Anywhere to get away from his humdrum existence in that back of beyond smallholding. He craved adventure before he got too old. There was nothing to hold him back, he convinced himself. Maybe he could get to Australia if he went backpacking. He could get work on the sheep stations and maybe get a place in a couple of years if he was careful. He wouldn't tell Norma if he decided to go. He didn't want her tagging along. On the other hand, if he did the dirty on her she may shoot her mouth off and he would be dragged back to face charges. No, he would have to take her and maybe get rid of her in the outback somewhere. He'd read about people disappearing in the outback and never being found. He would just tell her family that she had walked out on him. Yes, that might be a plan. He made his way home to see if Jenny had left him anything to eat.

Over the next few months news of the robbery seemed to have died down. Mick carried on, as usual, working by day and spending his nights down at the pub with Norma. He and Jenny seemed to be getting along better. They avoided one another if possible and she had not taken a beating for a couple of months now. Mick didn't seem as moody. He was surprisingly quite civil to her when they met up. She was only glad the girls didn't have to witness the violence. He still made Jenny's skin crawl if he even touched her. She just wished he would disappear one day and never come back.

Tom was so relieved they had not been caught. No one around had any inkling about what he had been up to. In the eyes of the local community, he was a hard-working respectable ex-military man with a lovely wife and family. As Cathie reflected later, she had no inkling either. She was so happy then. The business was picking up. Tom was working hard. The eldest children were doing well in school. Neil had joined the local Rugby team and Sarah attended dance classes. Normal village life. Never in a million years would Cathie have dreamed what the future held in store for them all.

Chapter Fourteen

Tom had not set eyes on Mick in months. He avoided the Red Dragon. He didn't pursue the money Mick would make from the sale of the cigarettes.

I'll let sleeping dogs lie. The less I see of that brother-in-law of mine the better. Tom had bought an old Riley Victor saloon car from one of his customers. It had been sitting in his garage since before the war and Tom and the owner came to an agreement over wavering a garage bill along with part cash from the business. Tom was pleased with the deal. He had spent a lot of time refurbishing his project and now the car was in pristine condition.

"We'll get a tidy sum for this one at the classic auctions," he told Cathie excitedly as he proudly showed her the car. "It's quite a sought-after model." Cathie was very impressed.

"We'll take the kids and go to the auctions together," she suggested. "Good idea," replied Tom. "I think this is the way to make money, Cathie. Not relying on fiddling little council contracts who could let us down at any moment. We'll get rid of a couple of the minibuses and buy project cars with the money."

"At last," sighed Cathie. "You have got your business head on. Classic cars are worth more than money in the bank. Oh, I do love you, Tom."

"Love you too Cathie. I am sorry I 've been such a pig-headed know it all in the past. We'll be all right now and get some of this mortgage paid off."

As Tom predicted, the Riley made a very good profit and with some of the money, Tom bought a battered old Morris Minor with a split windscreen he had spotted earlier. As they loaded her on to the trailer Tom winked at Cathie.

"Soon get this old girl spick and span and looking like new. Can't wait to start working on her."

Cathie remembered the day she and Jenny had made arrangements to do some shopping and have lunch in the local town. Jenny had rung her up and asked her sister to go for lunch, just the two of them.

"I have something to tell you," Jenny told her. Cathie was intrigued and a bit worried.

'I hope she isn't pregnant' she thought to herself. 'Not with all the trouble we had when Mick didn't get the son he wanted'. The girls were coming over and Tom had volunteered to keep an eye on all the children and give them dinner and tea.

Jenny arrived in her battered old pick up and Cathie gave her sister a cuddle.

"It's a lovely Spring day and we 're going to have a good time. Shall we take my car? It's a bit roomier than yours." Jenny laughed.

"No need to be that tactful, Cathie. I did mean to clean all the mud off before I came over, but time ran out. But yes, it will be nice to be chauffeured around." As they got into her car Cathie remarked.

"Why we don't do this more often I don't know," Jenny smiled.

"It wouldn't be so special then. We are both busy people. I

hardly have a minute to myself and the weeks just fly by." They set off down the road to town and Cathie couldn't wait to ask the question.

"Well, what have you got to tell me our Jenny. I've been thinking all sorts. Just tell me you're not pregnant again." Jenny laughed.

"Fat chance of that even if I wanted it. It takes two to tango and I don't fancy my so-called husband anymore and I think the feeling is mutual." She shuddered.

"Ok then," Cathie sounded relieved. "But what is it? Don't keep me guessing." Jenny smiled.

"Let's enjoy some shopping and I'll tell you over lunch." Cathie had to be satisfied with that.

Cathie bought trousers and tops for the boys and a dress for Sarah.

"They grow out of clothes so quickly," she remarked. "I only bought them trousers six months ago."

"Same here," answered Jenny. "I'll get jeans for my girls. Much more practical on the smallholding. They both help me a lot now. Especially Dilys. She loves animals and sits with the sheep or the chickens if one of them is sick, she wants to be a vet when she is older but that costs money. I can't see Mick agreeing to her going to university. He would want her to leave school and start earning as soon as possible. He has no interest at all in what the girls want."

Cathie felt sorry for her sister and tried to cheer her up.

"Things may change Jenny. You never know what's around the corner." Jenny nodded and smiled.

"You're right, Cathie. We should do this more often. You keep me positive."

"Believe me, I've had a lot of practice at keeping positive. I have nearly taken to the drink on many an occasion. If it weren't for the kids, I think I would have joined up again. But thankfully things seem to have taken a turn for the better lately."

"Same here, funnily enough, Cathie," said Jenny. "Mick and I don't row so much. Maybe that's because we hardly see one another anymore. He has other interests."

"I have heard rumours," said Cathie. "Do you want to talk about it?"

"Over lunch," replied Jenny. "Come on, I've done shopping. Have you? There's a pub over there advertising lunches. Let's go and look at the menu."

Over lunch, Jenny confided in Cathie that Mick had been unfaithful to her practically from the start of their marriage. Cathie sat silent and listened. She knew the gossip about Mick must be true but she and Tom had decided not to interfere. It was none of their business. It would only make things worse and Mick would do what he wanted anyway. He was not family orientated.

As Jenny was on her second glass of red wine, she opened up a bit more to her sister.

"Oh Cathie, at first I was brokenhearted. I adored Mick and thought we would live happily ever after. I was a naive little kid. You did try to tell me but I went ahead and got pregnant. I got what I deserved. Mick resented being tied down so young to me and the kids. Over the years I have hardened myself to the fact that I would never have a marriage like yours and Tom's. You are so lucky. Tom loves you. Mick only loves himself or whatever bit of skirt is conveniently around at the time. He uses people." She managed to curb her tongue when it came to telling her sister about the beatings. She was too ashamed.

"At least I have two lovely girls from the sham of a marriage. That is something to be thankful for. I am just letting off steam Cathie. It's probably the wine. Usually, I just bottle things up. Let's have a pudding and a coffee and then go and sit in the park. I still have something else to tell you."

"I know," said Cathie. "I can't imagine what it is that is so secret."

"It's nothing bad Cathie but I think you will be surprised."

After lunch, they headed over to the park. They sat on a bench near the lake and watched the children throwing bread for the ducks. Jenny sat silent. Cathie started the conversation as Jenny was making no effort to talk.

"Do you think you will stay on the smallholding, Jenny? I worry about your future sometimes. It's such hard work. You are out in all weathers." Jenny turned to her sister.

"But I love it there Cathie. It's my life now. Growing vegetables for the market with the children helping. It is hard work especially on market days but I enjoy it."

"Well, you do look fit and well Jenny, I must say. The outdoor life must suit you. It doesn't seem to bother you that Mick has another woman."

"To be honest Cathie, we are all much happier when he is not around. He can stay away as much as he likes." She hesitated and started to say something then stopped.

"What is it, Jenny? What's wrong?" Jenny looked at her sister.

"Nothing's wrong. In fact, it's just the opposite. Don't be annoyed, Cathie. I know I am breaking my wedding vows but I have met someone else." She waited for Cathie's reaction.

"Well, that's the last thing I would have thought of." Cathie was taken aback. "Who is he, where did you meet him and how long has this been going on?"

Jenny told Cathie she had met him at the market. He mended and sold second-hand farm and gardening tools. He began to help her unload her vegetables from her pick up and from there they got to chatting and having coffee together. His stall was next to hers. He had a smallholding too so they had a lot in common. He was single. Never married. He lived in an isolated valley about five miles away from Jenny. He was forty years old and his name was Gwilym. Jenny took a breath and waited for a reaction.

"I wonder why he never married?" was Cathie's first question. Jenny answered.

"I thought you would ask that. I asked the same thing. Gwilym told me he had inherited the smallholding and had lived with his parents all his life. He never mixed much socially. One or two girls he did have an interest in were not interested in his way of life and he did not want to change his lifestyle so things just didn't work out for him. When his parents died, he was just content running the smallholding and his market stall and chatting to friends on market days. He says he wishes he had met a woman like me years ago."

She paused.

"Please don't make another mistake Jenny. Take things

slowly."

Cathie was remembering the last time she gave Jenny advice and that she totally ignored it. She hoped this time she would listen. Jenny did not comment and then carried on telling Cathie about Gwilym.

"He is so kind and thoughtful, Cathie. I have never had that from a man. After putting up with Mick all these years I really appreciate a bit of kindness. We have known each other for six months now and I've never been happier. He knows about Mick and that I have two children. I have been up to his place on non-market days. It's a very pretty spot and he owns it. Not like me, having to pay rent each month. He seems very serious about going further with the relationship but we have to keep everything secret. I don't know how Mick would react. He may be relieved that I have someone else or he may go the other way and threaten to kill him. I just don't know what to do now."

Cathie was quite shocked. She knew Jenny was unhappy in her marriage but she never in her wildest dreams imagined her sister having an affair.

"I knew there was something different about you Jenny. You look happier. I just thought it was because you and Mick were getting on better these days. Are you sure you are doing the right thing? Someone always gets hurt in these situations and I don't want it to be you."

"I know Cathie. I don't want to make another mistake either. I'm trying to slow things down a bit but I think I am falling for Gwilym. It's because of his kindness towards me. I have never had that in all the years I have been married to Mick. Since our wedding night, he has been nothing but cruel and sarcastic towards me. I stopped loving him a long time ago and I know it's the same for him. I just wish he would disappear somewhere and I could be free to have someone of my own who will love me for just being me. I am sure the girls would not miss their father. They see how unhappy he makes me."

Cathie took her sister's hand.

"I am so sorry you ended up with a bad marriage Jenny, but just bide your time. If it's meant to be it will happen. Let's see if Mick makes a move and then he can't throw any guilt in your face. From what I have heard around the garage, this Norma woman is digging her claws into him quite deep. She is talking of marriage and babies. Maybe he will go and you will get your freedom without lifting a finger. Just bide your time."

"Good thinking," agreed Jenny. "I'll try and be patient to make sure I am doing the right thing. I'm glad I have told you. I hate keeping secrets from you. Come on shall we head back. It's starting to get quite chilly."

Chapter Fifteen

One Saturday evening Mick and Norma were sat in the corner of the pub as usual. Norma was in a thoroughly bad mood.

"I'm sick of all your promises and dreams Mick," she began. "When we got together you promised me that we would go to Australia and start a new life in the sun. I helped you steal money from the shop. I believed you. Now here we are two years later, still sitting in this dingy pub supping pints. You keep on promising and nothing ever happens. You're just a dreamer. I'm sorry I ever helped you in the first place. I've a good mind to tell the cops what you did. I don't care anymore. I'll only get a telling off. I didn't do the robbery. I'm fed up with working there anyway."

"Don't be stupid, Norma," retorted Mick. "What's brought this on? You'll go to jail for what you did, don't you know that? You'll never get another job around here."

"Well, I'm just fed up," answered Norma. "I trusted you and you have let me down. No wonder your wife doesn't want you. You're just a waster." Mick didn't like what he was hearing. The last thing he wanted was for Norma to blow the whistle on him. That would spoil his plans for the rest of his life. A convicted criminal would not be accepted in Australia or Europe for that matter. He would be stuck here forever. He had to think quick.

He turned on the charm.

"Don't be like that darling," he began. "I love you. I need to be with you. I am saving hard for our future. I am working all the hours I can get. You know that. The only free time I have I spend it with you. I hate us to be apart. I am not a waster. It's just that I want things to be right for us when we do emigrate. I don't want you scrimping and scraping and having to go out to work. I want you to be a proper wife to me, looking after the house and just being there when I get home from work. Maybe we could have a couple of kids. What do you say? Do you understand how I feel?" He held her hand across the table and looked into her eyes. "I love you very much and always will. I have never felt this way about any other woman. *'My God, Mick. You should get an Oscar for this.* He sounded so convincing.

Norma had taken the bait. She squeezed his hand and smiled.

"I'm sorry Mick, for doubting you. I was just in a bad mood. I've had a row with my Mum and just took it out on you. I would never shop you. I want more than anything for us to be married and have children. Why do we have to go to Australia to do that?"

Mick hesitated then explained. "It's just that I was trapped at seventeen into a marriage I wasn't ready for. I have always dreamed of going to live in Australia. It's becoming an obsession. If I don't do it before I have any more children I will never go. Just be a little more patient with me Norma. Give me another twelve months to get the money together. In a few months, we will apply for our visas, I promise you with all my heart."

Norma was now totally convinced that she would be on her way to Australia in twelve months, to a new land, husband and a family to look forward to. She went home a very happy woman that evening, and Mick breathed a huge sigh of relief.

He had another robbery planned. He had not been idle, and had been cruising around various petrol stations further out of the area. He eventually chooses one about fifty miles away from the last one he had robbed. He thought that would be enough distance for the police not to suspect a connection.

He called in for petrol over the next few weeks at various times of the day. He was determined this time not to make any mistakes. He needed to make sure of the manager's hours so he would have access to the safe and to pray that nothing would happen that would mean the manager taking the day off. He would just pull out and not attempt the robbery if the manager was not on site. He planned a mid-morning hit. He made a mental note that this was the quietest time. Now he needed to break the news to Tom.

Tom was underneath a car repairing the exhaust when he heard a voice that he had been dreading to hear. Work had picked up and the business was solvent again. He did not need to hear Mick's voice.

"Hi, Tom, how you doing? Long time no see."

"Hi, Mick," Tom slid out from underneath the car. "I've been pretty busy. The business has picked up at last."

"Good to hear that," replied Mick. "Let's have a drink together and a catch-up." Tom hesitated.

"I'm up to my eyes in work this week Mick, I don't know if I can spare the time."

"Good for you but I was looking forward to a couple of pints and a chat. Never mind, sometime soon eh? By the way, I saw Megan's old man the other day. He seemed a bit upset. Said he had something that Cathie needed to know and if I saw her would I tell her to give him a ring. Is she in the office Tom or at home? I would like to see her as well. Haven't seen her in ages. Is Megan still working for you?" Tom felt the threat of blackmail once again in Mick's voice.

Will he always have that hold over me? Cathie can't find out about me and Megan. It would destroy us and I would lose everything. What a foolish bastard I've been. If only I could turn the clock back.

"Ok Mick, I get the drift," sneered Tom. "I'll be in the Red Dragon on Thursday night." Tom slid back under the car he was working on.

"Ok Tom, I see you are busy. See you Thursday. Be like old times." He grinned to himself as he got back into his van.

As Mick and Tom settled in the corner of the bar, Tom knew what was coming. His stomach was churning. He felt sick. One of these days they were bound to get caught. Mick had kept most of the money from the cigarette sales from the last robbery. Tom had not asked for his cut and Mick had not volunteered it.

"Norma has been on my back about emigrating and having kids, Tom. You know what women are like when they get something stuck in their heads. They never let it go. She keeps on and on about the promises I have made to her. Daft bitch. But she does have a bit of a hold over us. I want to keep her sweet for your sake as well as mine. You do understand, don't you Tom?"

"Oh, I understand all right," replied Tom sarcastically. "You and her are tarred with the same brush. You'll do anything to get your own way, even resorting to blackmail. Loyalty means nothing." Mick looked shocked.

"Blackmail, that's a very dirty word."

"Accept it, Mick, that's what you are doing. You wouldn't hesitate to blab off to Cathie if I didn't dance to your tune and don't you deny it. And now Norma is doing the same to you." He laughed. Mick was on the defensive.

"It's not as if you don't get something out of this Tom. I take all the risks."

"I wish we had never started down this road," replied Tom.

"Easy to say that now, isn't it Tom? When your business is doing good. Remember when you didn't know where the next penny was coming from and the bills were piling up around your ears and the business was on the brink of bankruptcy. Remember those times Tom. Remember who showed you a way out."

"Ok Mick, point taken," replied Tom. "I know what's coming, so let's get on with it, where and when."

Mick named the garage he had picked out and the time to hit it.

"What if someone pulls in for petrol and goes in to pay?" asked Tom.

"I've thought of all that," answered Mick. "I've gone over and over in my mind the 'what ifs'. If someone pulls on to the forecourt whilst I am inside you will have to stall them. Pretend you're having trouble starting your car or tell them you have seen smoke coming from their car. You'll think of something. Anything to stall them. I have checked they have a closed sign as well which you can put across the entrance. That will put most people off. I have checked the times of the day when it's less busy. I won't be inside that long. Also, because it's daylight we don't want anyone to recognize us. We can wear big coats and caps. I can buy a pair of glasses with clear lenses and I thought you could grow a beard. Shave it off afterwards. Tell Cathie you fancy seeing what you look like with a beard. We can both do Scouse accents with a bit of practice. That may throw the police off the scent. They'll think it's a gang from Liverpool that's done over the garage. We can get rid of the car the same way as before. Job done."

"Fair enough," sighed Tom. "You seem to have done your homework better this time. Seems you have covered everything. I take it there's no alarm system to the cop shop or a guard dog tucked away somewhere."

"No, I 've checked all that out," replied Mick. "Anyway, the nearest police station to there, is twenty miles away. I can cut all the phone wires before I go in. I know where they are. Shall we say in about two weeks then Tom?" asked Mick. "I'll see you in here next week same time to finalize everything."

"Ok, I suppose so," muttered Tom. "Let's get it over with and I hope to God this is the last time. The day you and Norma get on that ship for Australia I will come and wave you off."

They met as planned the following Thursday. Tom already had quite a growth of beard.

"Does Cathie like the beard," asked Mick.

"No, she does not," replied Tom, "She says it's like kissing a lavatory brush." Mick grinned.

"Ah well, It's only for another week. Then you can shave it all off. It doesn't suit you I must admit, but it will do the job next week."

"Good," said Tom, "I hate it. I feel all itchy and scruffy."

Over their drinks, they finalized their plans. Tom would provide the car as usual with false plates and pick-up Mick on the day planned. If they did be unfortunate enough to encounter someone else on the forecourt, they would soon have the police on their tail with a description of the car. They discussed this and Mick decided that they should drive straight to his smallholding and hide the car in his barn initially and drive Tom back to his garage. Tom would shave and tell Cathie he couldn't stand her moaning about the beard any longer then go back to work. He would make up some story of where he had been for the morning.

Later that evening Tom would meet Mick in the pub. They would drive back over to the smallholding and pick up the car and that night Tom would respray it and put the original number plates back on. He would explain to Phil and Cathie that he needed to get it done that night as he had a buyer for it the next day who wanted a car urgently. He would then take the car back to Mick's and they would get rid of it at the next auction. So many lies.

"Won't Jenny wonder why cars keep coming and going?" inquired Tom.

"If she says anything, I'll tell her you are doing a bit of tax dodging. She won't think anything of it. Too busy with her own life to bother with what we are doing. Don't worry about her."

Mick thought to himself 'If she does start asking questions, I'll just give her a good belting. That will shut her up'.

D day arrived and they set off for the garage. Tom parked the car around the side pretending to check his tyre pressures as

Mick strolled casually into the garage. As he spotted the cashier and the manager chatting, he pulled out a gun.

"Open the safe," he growled. "And if you touch anything, you're a dead 'un," he threatened the cashier. "Put your hands on the counter." Shaking the woman did as she was told. The manager had gone a deathly waxy colour.

"Be bloody quick about it, I haven't got all day," shouted Mick, pushing the gun into the manager's ribs. He hurried to open the safe and fumbled with the combination as quickly as his shaking hands would let him. "Now fill the bag with the notes and yer won't get hurt," instructed Mick in a broad Liverpool twang. When he had the bag of money Mick shouted at the two of them to lie down on the floor.

". If you try to ring the police, I will shoot you dead," he snarled waving the gun. He backed out of the garage and quickly jumped into the car.

"Well, that was the easiest few grand we have ever earned for a morning's work." He slapped Tom on the back as they sped away. "That manager nearly shit himself when he saw the gun and it was only a dummy," he laughed.

"A gun," Tom was horrified. "You never mentioned a gun. Dummy or not. We'd have been banged up for years if things had gone the wrong way."

"Well, they didn't did they? Don't be so negative Tom. Things have gone our way for once. We are getting good at this. It's better than slogging our guts out to earn a living." Tom glanced over at him.

"This is the last time Mick. I mean it. Our luck will run out sometime. You surely have enough now to do what you want. I think I will take Cath and the kids on holiday with my share. We've never had a holiday since we've had the business. I can always tell her I've been salting a bit out of the takings each week to pay for it."

"Good idea," agreed with Mick. "Mine will go straight into my Australia pot."

When they arrived at Mick's place Tom suggested hiding the money and splitting it at a later date. Mick nodded.

"Let's get you and me back to work as soon as. Then no one will ask too many questions as to where we have been."

Cathie was surprised to see Tom appear at the house and into the bathroom.

"I can't stand this beard any longer," he shouted to her. "What with you moaning and one of the customer's telling me I look twenty years older. It's coming off."

"You could have waited till you'd finished work," answered Cathie puzzled.

"No, have to go out straight after work," he shouted back. "One of our customers wants a car urgently by tomorrow. Don't know what time I 'll be home. Don't wait up love." Cathie was used to Tom's comings and goings. She just had to trust him. And she did, she told herself.

Two weeks went by. They kept an eye on the news and as they had predicted the police assumed the criminals had driven over from Liverpool thinking country garages were easy pickings. The car had been auctioned off and Tom was awaiting Mick to contact him regarding his share of the money. In the end, he had to catch up with Mick on one of the nights he knew he would be seeing Norma.

"Hi Tom," called Mick from the bar. "I was coming over to the garage tomorrow to see you."

"Convenient," answered Tom sarcastically. "I wonder if you would have come if I hadn't seen you tonight."

"Don't be like that Tom. Meet me in the Fox and Hounds in town on Thursday night and we can have a catch-up. I'm a bit tied up tonight," he said nodding towards Norma.

On Thursday night they met up as planned.

"Where's my money," demanded Tom as soon as they had sat down.

"Easy Tom, don't you trust me?" asked Mick.

"As far as I could throw you," retorted Tom.

"I have your money here with me," said Mick sounding hurt. He quickly passed a packet under the table.

"How much is there?" demanded Tom.

"One thousand and five hundred notes," answered Mick in a low voice.

"What?" Tom was sure he must have misheard. "You must have taken three times that much."

"Keep your voice down Tom. People are turning to look at us. I am being honest with you Tom. I wouldn't cheat you. Surely you know that. When I counted it up, there was only three grand altogether. I swear on Jenny's life."

"Well, that doesn't convince me much. You hate her guts. You couldn't give a toss if you never saw her again."

"Well, it's true anyway. I split it fifty-fifty, on my life."

"I don't believe you, Mick," said Tom. "But I can't bloody well prove it either. You've got me over a barrel."

"Come on Tom, we're partners, aren't we? I wouldn't do the dirty on you. You know it." Tom was not convinced. He stood up.

"I'm off home. We have done what we came to do. I hope that's the end of it."

"Well, I'll stay and have another pint," said Mick. "I've nothing to go home to." As Tom disappeared out of the door Mick smiled to himself.

Well, who takes all the risks? He doesn't deserve a fifty-fifty cut. Just one more job and Bye-bye Britain. I think I will treat myself to a whisky to celebrate.

Chapter Sixteen

"Hi Cathie, are you free for lunch?"

Jenny sounded happy and excited as she chatted to her sister on the phone.

"You sound in a good mood, Jenny. Must be that new man of yours," Cathie whispered down the phone.

"I must admit he has brought me back to believing in myself again," laughed Jenny. "I'm not a drudge and a burden around someone's neck as Mick would have me believe. Anyway, enough of that unfeeling low-life that I married. Come out to lunch and we can have a good catch up."

"Sounds just what I need," answered Cathie. "I'll just switch the phone over to the garage and I'll meet you in town about one."

The sisters met up and ordered lunch in their favourite pub.

"Gosh, we haven't done this in ages," Cathie began. "Not since you dropped the bombshell about your secret affair. How's it going?"

"I couldn't be happier Cathie. Gwilym makes me feel so special and alive. He helps me on the market stall as well. Sometimes we take the girls out for a ride and fish and chips. They wouldn't tell their Dad. I have no fear of that. Mick has never taken any interest in them or taken them out anywhere. To tell you the truth, Gwilym is more of a Dad to them." They paused as their meals arrived.

"Go on Jenny," urged Cathie sensing that Jenny was in the

mood to unburden herself of all she was feeling.

"The girls get on really well with Gwilym and I can spend a bit more time with them now as I have help on the stall. They do seem happier."

"It's a pity you have that sod of a husband in the way or you could all move in together and be a real family," remarked Cathie.

"I'm so glad you see it from my point of view and not judge me for breaking my wedding vows," answered Jenny sounding relieved. "I'll tell you now why I've turned to someone else. To tell you the whole truth, I've had a pretty rotten life with Mick. I've never told anyone before as I was too ashamed but I will tell you something that will shock you." She took a deep breath. "He's beaten me almost senseless on many an occasion. He's vicious when he gets going. I was too humiliated to tell anyone, not even you. I would make the girls run down the field and hide if he came home in a temper but many a time Annie would try to stop him hitting me. He didn't care if she got in the way when he was like that. He made our lives hell. When he had driven off in his van or gone up to bed, the girls would sit by me till I got myself together. It was like living through a nightmare and I told the girls not to tell anyone."

"Why couldn't you tell us, Jenny love?" Tears were rolling down Cathie's face.

"I was too ashamed, Cathie. You told me not to marry him and thank God he never hurt the kids. I was just kind of existing hoping that things would get better. And after a while, they seemed to. I don't know if it was because that Norma kept him calmer or I think it was maybe because the girls are getting older. Annie told him after he knocked me about a few months ago that if he ever touched her mother again, she would go straight to the police. She would too. I reckon he'd think twice about hitting me now. I just wish he and that woman would go away somewhere together. I could manage on my own. I would run my stall and get a part-time job now the children are older. If only I could get rid of him."

Cathie blew her nose and wiped her eyes when Jenny had finished speaking. Their meal lay untouched.

"I never realized he was beating you." Cathie sounded shocked. "I knew he had a temper and could be verbally abusive. I never had much to do with him if he came to see Tom. There was always something about him I didn't like. I know what it was now. I only wish I had known sooner."

"Well at first it wasn't so bad, he just used to say nasty things to me and punch me occasionally but after Dilys was born he got really abusive. He wanted a boy you see, and said it was all my fault that we'd had another girl. The least little thing seemed to send him over the edge. I was so ashamed that I couldn't stand up to him. That is why I didn't tell anyone. I just tried to keep me and the kids out of his way as much as possible." Cathie shook her head. She was lost for words.

"Come on Jenny, let's eat this lunch before it gets cold. It looks very nice." Jenny smiled as she began to eat.

"Things haven't been as bad lately, honest Cathie. Don't upset yourself. I just wanted you to know why I have found someone who really loves me and I don't feel worthless anymore. I feel strong enough to stand up to Mick now if he started."

"You make me feel very guilty, our Jenny," said Cathie. "I

married a wonderful man who would do anything for me and the children and here's you married to an absolute bastard."

"Luck of the draw, Cathie. Marriage is a lottery. You don't know anyone 'till you live with them. You are lucky to have found your Tom though. Serves me right for getting into trouble with the first boy who ever showed any interest in me. You had lots of choices in the Army I expect." She looked enquiringly over at her sister.

"Well yes," Cathie admitted. "There were a few boyfriends but I knew Tom was the one as soon as I went out with him. I suppose I just got to know blokes a bit better than you. But you have a good one now by the sound of it."

"I believe I have," agreed Jenny. "But I'm not going to rush into things. Once bitten, twice shy. If we still feel the same in twelve months and Mick is still around, I'm going to go for a divorce. I've made my mind up that I won't be tied to that pig forever."

"Good for you," said Cathie, "but I'm glad you are taking your time. You don't want to make any more mistakes, and promise me you won't keep secrets from me anymore."

"I promise Cathie, on my life. I will tell you if Mick starts on me again."

Mick and Norma were sitting in their usual spot in the Red Dragon. By now everyone knew of the affair going on between them. It was all out in the open and Mick had told all his mates that his wife knew and didn't care. In fact, he informed them she would be glad to see the back of him. The marriage had finished a while ago. This information suited Norma. She had big plans for her and Mick. She loved him, and their future with him and a family was her favourite topic of conversation.

"When you get your divorce Mick, we can get married straight away," she began. "I want two kids and I don't want to wait till I am too old to enjoy them." She hesitated. "You do want kids don't you Mick?" Mick smiled at her.

"Of course, darling. We will bring them up in Australia. The best place on earth to bring up children. We'll get a house by the beach and we can all learn to swim and surf in all that hot sunny weather. It will be perfect." She smiled and cuddled up to him.

Good job she's not a mind reader. Mick smiled at her and stroked her thigh. *I'll put up with her for a while when we emigrate and see her settled in a job. Then I'll be off. She's ok in the sack, but I certainly don't want any more kids at my age. I don't enjoy the ones I've got.*

"You're quiet Mick. Are you thinking about Australia?" Norma enquired.

"You must have read my mind, Norma love," he answered. "We have nearly enough stashed away to be on our way and leave this dreary old country behind us. Just have a little more patience for me to tie up a few loose ends here."

"I'm so excited Mick. I can't breathe sometimes when I think about it. I can't wait to get on the ship. I've been buying some summer clothes and packing them away for the trip. I hope we can go by the end of the year. It will be coming into their summer then."

"I'm sure we will be able to make it by then, my darling," answered Mick. "But don't go blabbing your mouth off about our plans and telling everyone. Not even your family," he warned her, thoughts of child maintenance running through his head.

"I won't Mick," she promised.

Mick was planning just one more job. A big one that would fund a decent truck when they reached Australia. He had enough saved for the fare and rent to keep them until they both managed to get jobs. He would have to call on Tom's services one more time.

He called round to Tom and Cathie's house the next Sunday morning. Cathie saw him coming and she remembered how much she loathed him for how he had treated her sister. She didn't want to confront him that morning. She knew he would only take it out on Jenny if he knew Jenny had been discussing their situation. Also, she had not told Tom as she knew he would confront Mick and all hell would be let loose. She disappeared into the kitchen and hoped Tom would not invite him in.

Tom was in the garden planting some runner beans.

"Hi Tom, she's keeping you busy I see," Mick called. Tom reluctantly stopped what he was doing to talk to him.

"What do you want?"

"You don't seem very pleased to see me, Tom. Is Cathie in?"

"She is but she's busy." Tom knew Cathie hated Mick coming round. He could feel the atmosphere. He assumed it was because she knew Mick was cheating on her sister.

"Just go in and tell her I want you to look at the pickup, will you? I want to ask you something." Tom could guess it would be nothing he would welcome hearing, but he knew he had no choice, so he disappeared into the house to tell Cathie he was going out for a while.

"I'll give you a lift to the pub," called Mick. Reluctantly Tom climbed into the pickup and they made their way to the Red Dragon.

Chapter Seventeen

Once again, over a pint Mick informed Tom that he had another job planned and he would need a getaway car.

"When is all this going to end?" demanded Tom. "We have been lucky enough so far to get away with what we have but do we have to push our luck any further? Haven't you got enough stashed away yet to do your disappearing act?" Tom was really angry.

"Keep your voice down," warned Mick. "You are drawing attention to yourself. To answer your question, yes, I have got enough stashed away but I just need enough for a truck to set me up right when I get there and they don't come cheap. We plan to go late Autumn and you will be shut of me for good then. Not a word to Cathie mind or it will go straight back to Jenny."

"I would expect Jenny would think all her birthdays had come at once if you disappeared, Mick, and all her prayers answered as well," added Tom sarcastically.

"Don't be like that Tom. Jenny would miss me if I left." He sounded hurt and Tom looked at him in astonishment.

"You really have a high opinion of yourself haven't you Mick?" "I understand women Tom," replied Mick. "Women like a bad guy. Stops them getting bored. Cathie should know more about what you get up to." Mick looked at Tom slyly.

"Cathie and I are rock solid, thank you," replied Tom. "I think even if you tried telling her about Megan, I don't think she would believe you. You can't hurt me anymore Mick."

"Well," said Mick. "You do surprise me. I will have to find someone else to get a car for me. What about Phil? I am sure he will be tempted with the thought of a few grand in the bank. He must struggle on the wages you give him with all his brood to feed. Or what about that young lad you've just taken on. What's his name? Jimmy isn't it. He's got a driving license. I could ask him."

"Don't you go asking them to do your dirty work. They're good lads." retorted Tom. "They would have to involve the garage anyway."

"Come on Tom, we are partners in this. I don't really want anyone else involved. I trust you. I was only messing. Just one more job. It's easy money. I'm sure your business could do with another injection of cash and you know by now how to filter it in. You wouldn't have to work so hard to meet the bills. More time with Cathie and the kids."

Tom was tempted. Quite often he was working such long hours he never saw his children for more than a few minutes each day. It would be nice to spend more time with his family before they grew much older. The jobs they had done had been easy so far.

"Let me think it over Mick," said Tom. "I'm off home now for my dinner. I'll let you know."

"Don't be taking too long," called Mick. "Or I'll be having a word with Phil, and he may put two and two together as to why you bought cars and sold them a couple of days later when we had robberies in the area. All it would take is a whisper in his ear from someone and I think the penny would drop."

"There you go again with the threats," Tom sounded angry.

"That is pure blackmail. I will be so glad when you are on the other side of the world. I will let you know by Thursday."

Tom mulled over his dilemma during the next few days. Would one more robbery be too much to chance? It would make a big difference to the business. He could filter in the money gradually and buy the classic car project he had been eyeing up for the past couple of months. It would really make a difference to his family. The more he thought about it the more positive he became. At the back of his mind was the worry that Phil might find out what he had been up to and tell Cathie. There was no danger that Phil would let Mick persuade him to do anything dishonest. Phil was as straight and honest as anyone he knew. Tom could not bear the shame of Phil finding out. He couldn't take the risk. Mick had backed him into a corner once again through his own stupidity.

He caught up with Mick in the Red Dragon the next Thursday evening.

"I'm in for the last time," Tom informed him.

"I thought you might see it my way," grinned Mick. "I promise you it will be the very last time. I'll be gone before Christmas."

"I'm counting on it," replied Tom.

A few days later, Tom, Phil and Jimmy were sat in the garage having a well-earned tea break.

"Business is getting better Phil, thank the Lord," remarked Tom. "But we do need a few more contracts if we are to keep going next year."

"You do surprise me Tom," answered Phil. "We seem to be

doing ok and we have two classics in the back waiting for renovation. They will make a good profit. I realize they take time to bring them up to pristine condition. Meantime the diary is quite full. You're a born worrier Tom. You will be a millionaire by the time you're forty. Mark my words." Tom laughed and turned to Jimmy.

"You are very quiet Jimmy. Are you settling in here alright?" asked Tom, concerned that the lad seemed unhappy.

"It's got to be women trouble," said Phil. "That's the only thing that would put an expression like that on a blokes' face."

"I'm ok," replied Jimmy. "I'll go and start valeting the Merc you've just repaired," and he put down his tea and walked back into the garage.

"There's definitely something up with him," said Phil. "Jimmy was as happy as Larry last week, chatting away like a parrot on speed, he was. Now I can't get a word out of him. I'll choose my moment and find out what is wrong with him. It's not work, I'm sure."

Over the next couple of days Phil waited for an opportunity to find out what was wrong. One evening after a particularly busy day Phil suggested he and Jimmy go over to the Red Dragon for a pint.

"The wife's gone to visit her mother," he explained to Jimmy. "I don't have to get home straight away tonight. I'm let off the leash so I'm going to the pub, and some company would be good."

"It's a woman isn't it?" Phil came straight to the point as they sat by the bar. "Tom and I hate to see you so quiet. Tom thinks he's upset you."

"Well, he hasn't, so please put him straight. The truth is Phil, I don't know what to do. I can't talk to my parents. They wouldn't understand."

"Well try me," encouraged Phil. "I do know a bit about women you know." He smiled at Jimmy who was now on his second pint and was in the mood to talk.

"I met a wonderful girl in a club in Chester about two months ago. We really hit it off and I thought she was the one, Phil. I can't stop thinking about her. I've had loads of girlfriends but this one is really special." Phil was intrigued.

"What happened then Jimmy, have you finished with her?"

"I don't really know, that's the problem," replied Jimmy. "She has just stopped answering the phone when I try to ring her. Some other woman always answers and says she is out. I don't know what I have done wrong." Jimmy looked really upset. Phil thought for a moment. He felt sorry for the lad. If he was telling the truth and Phil believed he was, then this girl owed him an explanation.

"Maybe if you asked around where she works you may be able to find out something," suggested Phil.

"I suppose I could," replied Jimmy with little enthusiasm. "Perhaps she has just gone off me and I will have to face up to it."

"Well, you're young Jimmy. You have a good job and a nice car. You won't be on your own for long."

"Trouble is, I'm not interested Phil," sighed Jimmy. Phil looked at him. He wanted to help the lad. He found it uncomfortable working alongside this silent, unhappy young lad.

"What is her full name and where does she work, Jimmy?" enquired Phil.

"Her name is Marianne Maxwell and I think she works in one of those tall financial buildings down by the river in Chester. I believe she lives in a village a few miles from there called Seaton Hall. She mentioned it one night when we were talking. I have never been to her house. I have been travelling up to Chester to meet her. You would like her Phil. She is very pretty and very bubbly. We got on like a house on fire and even talked about the future together. Kids and everything. Then one night when we had arranged to meet, she didn't show up." He went quiet.

"Well, you seem to have landed yourself a good one there lad," commented Phil. "Not the local village girls you usually date. Not that there's anything wrong with them," he added hastily.

"That is exactly why she is special, Phil," explained Jimmy. "She is different and so interesting to talk too. She has travelled all over the place even though she is only twenty-one. She has been to America, Dubai, Nice, Italy. She tells some fascinating stories. What she is doing taking up with a grease monkey like me I've no idea."

"She must like a bit of rough, Jimmy," laughed Phil. "You must be very different from her usual boyfriends. If you are stuck on this girl, if it was me, I wouldn't settle without an explanation. You say there was nothing wrong between you and you were getting along fine. She may be ill or have family problems. Keep ringing her and if you get no joy go to those offices in Chester and make some enquiries. Nothing ventured, nothing gained. It's very strange she has suddenly dropped you like a stone."

Jimmy took Phil's advice. He rang again and to his surprise Marianne answered the phone.

"What's wrong?" Jimmy demanded as soon as he heard her voice.

"Why have you stopped seeing me? What have I done?" Before she had time to reply Jimmy heard a man's angry voice in the background and the phone went dead.

"Now I know there is something wrong," Jimmy muttered to himself. "She must be married. That must have been her husband in the background. What a fool I've been. I've a good mind to go to the place where she works and show her up for what she is." Jimmy was livid.

On his next day off Jimmy drove to Chester and parked up near the office block where he knew Marianne worked. He was still upset that she could have deceived him so easily. He walked into the building and enquired if a Marianne Maxwell worked there. The receptionist looked puzzled.

"Whose asking?" she enquired.

"She's a friend of mine," explained Jimmy. The receptionist looked him up and down.

"I find that very hard to believe," she told him. "And to answer your question, no Miss Maxwell does not work here. Her father Mr. Maxwell owns the business and he wouldn't be too pleased to have the likes of you keeping company with his daughter."

"Well, can you tell me where she lives please," persisted

Jimmy.

"Indeed, I can't," replied the receptionist sharply. "And you won't get to see her even if you find out. Her father employs minders to keep fortune hunters like you at bay. Now if you don't mind, I have work to do."

Jimmy was flabbergasted. He had no idea Marianne's family were rich. She had never spoken to him of her background. Now he understood why. She was not married as he had thought. It must have been her father or one of these 'minders' who had put the phone down on him that night. He relayed all this back to Phil at work the next day.

"Well Jimmy, that's what you get for punching above your weight," said Phil. "Has that solved the mystery now? Stick to the village girls in future. You know where you are with them."

Jimmy was not satisfied. He didn't want to give up so easily. There was also another side to persisting in this relationship. He smelled a good opportunity to improve his lifestyle. If he married Marianne his whole world would change. He told himself this was not money motivated. He had fallen for Marianne before he knew of her background. He would still love her if she didn't have a thing in the world. He loved her and he knew she loved him. She was over twenty-one and her father had no right in stopping them seeing one another. He would not give up on her. He spoke to Phil about his feelings.

"If you want to carry on with this relationship, you need to find out where she lives," advised Phil. "Then maybe catch up with her as she goes to the shops or something. And watch out for those minders. I don't want you lying in some alley, beaten to a pulp. You're playing a dangerous game, you know."

"It's not a game," Jimmy sounded exasperated. "I love her and I think she loves me and her father can't keep her locked up. He must have suspected something when she kept going to Chester every week and she has backed off now so as not to upset him. But I will take your advice and be extra careful Phil."

Tom was enquiring if Phil had found out why Jimmy was so distracted from his work.

"I have found out," answered Phil. "And we were right. It is a woman and he related the whole situation to Tom.

"Well, our Jimmy seems to have got himself tangled up in something he can't handle," smiled Tom. "Who would have thought it."

Mick was moody and agitated as he pushed the food around his plate one evening. The girls sat silently eating their dinner. They sensed his mood and didn't want to do anything to make him lash out at their mother. They had witnessed many such incidents. If their Dad was in a bad mood, he would send them upstairs and then they would hear shouting and banging. Dilys would start to shake and then wet herself. When they heard the door bang and then silence, they knew their father had gone out. Only then did they dare to run downstairs to check on their mother. Jenny put on a brave face in front of the girls but they knew she would be hurting. They had seen her bruises and black eyes on many occasions. They had witnessed her holding her ribs, struggling to lift boxes to take to market. They helped her where they could. They hated their father. Thank goodness these incidents were rare now since Annie had threatened her father with the police.

Dilys jumped as Mick scraped his chair to leave the table.

"I wouldn't feed that muck you give me to the pigs. I'm off out to get a decent meal. Don't wait up." They all sighed with relief as they heard Mick's van start up.

"I've got a lovely apple pie in the oven. "Jenny got up from the table. "We can enjoy it in peace now girls. We won't have to put up with him much longer, I hope. Gwilym and I hope to move in together soon and we can all live like a normal family without living in fear."

Mick was moody and agitated and hungry. He stopped off at the chip shop then drove off up a lane to eat his supper and to think. He had been toying with different ideas for his next planned robbery. He had thought about robbing the local bank but having looked into it further he abandoned the idea. There were too many complications. He had naively envisaged holding up the cashier. When he checked there were five cashiers to contend with and probably a panic button to the police station. He sensibly decided it was far too risky a commitment for amateur bank robbers and dropped the idea.

He had driven around the garages in the area and had his eye on one in particular. Again, it was distant from any police presence and he had studied when the manager was in or out of the building but he banked at different times of the day and night. Mick was not sure. He had discussed the plan with Tom.

"Well, if you don't have a good feeling about it then we shouldn't risk it. Our luck cannot hold out forever," advised Tom who was reluctant to break the law again anyway. His business was out of danger now.

"I've got to have money for the truck, "insisted Mick. "That bitch Norma is putting more and more pressure on me to set a date for Australia and I haven't got enough money. I'm desperate. I don't want all my plans to go down the pan." Tom was losing his temper.

"You are just too greedy," he told Mick. "You want everything handed to you on a plate. Why can't you just get a job when you get there and save for the truck like any decent man would do?"

"Too complicated," answered Mick. "I would be stuck with Norma for months and she keeps on about babies. The sooner I can get away from her the better."

"Why you couldn't make a go of it with your own wife is beyond me." Tom sounded annoyed. "Jenny is a good hard-working woman and an excellent mother but I will admit she will be far happier if you were on the other side of the world. That goes for the girls also, so I suppose we will have to come up with something for everyone's sake."

Mick was hanging around the garage more frequently, Cathie remembered. She became suspicious of his motives.

Why didn't she delve a bit deeper? She asked herself that question years later. 'Maybe I could have changed what happened'. But she trusted Tom even if she mistrusted Mick.

Mick was hoping Tom had come up with a plan. He was getting very impatient to get on with his future life and he was struggling with a plan for the next robbery. When he popped into the garage one afternoon, he overheard something that made him draw back from sight. A stroke of luck maybe?

Phil and Jimmy were discussing Jimmy's love interest.

"Any more info on that rich sugar babe of yours?" enquired Phil. Jimmy answered.

"I have found out where she lives and I went there. I had a big shock. She lives in a huge mansion of a place with electronic gates. A man was walking his dog and saw me hanging about outside. He told me that was where the millionaire lived. I got the impression her father wasn't too popular in the village. People were jealous I suppose. But no wonder he wants to keep me at bay. I expect he suspects every man who takes an interest in his daughter is a gold digger. I must admit though, marrying into that family would make a lot of my dreams come true."

"Be careful Jimmy," warned Phil. "The father sounds a ruthless buggar and money isn't everything is it? Make sure you take up with this girl for all the right reasons." Mick crept away from the garage without being seen. He now had a plan in mind.

Chapter Eighteen

Tom and Mick met in the Red Dragon that Thursday evening at Mick's request. Mick came straight to the point.

"A little bird has whispered in my ear that one of your staff is dating a millionaire's daughter. That's convenient isn't it," he sneered. Tom went quite cold.

"How do you know that?" he asked. "I don't want any of my staff involved in your dirty dealings."

"Hold on Tom, No one knows that I know. I haven't spoken to anybody in the garage. Give me credit for some discretion. But it's too good an opportunity not to investigate, don't you think?" Tom looked very uncomfortable.

"I am totally against this. I really don't want to be involved with you anymore."

"Now Tom, we've been over all this. By the way, I saw your Cathie the other day. She was looking very happy. We don't want to upset the apple-cart now do we? You only have to drive the car anyway. That's not much to ask for a cut of the stash now is it? You have the easy job, and then I'll be out of your life forever." Tom shifted uncomfortably in his seat. "There's Norma," said Mick. "Come and join us love," he called. "Tom hasn't seen you in ages. You can tell him all about our plans."

Tom had his instructions to find out what he could about Jimmy's girlfriend and her family. Reluctantly and discreetly, he complied. He made sure he sat down and had his tea breaks with Phil and Jimmy a few times a week. Jimmy now talked openly about his plans to see Marianne.

"I have found out that her Dad goes away quite a lot. He has companies in America and Canada. I know he is not at home at the moment. I think he is in America. I have written to Marianne and hope she gets the post before one of those minders or the housekeeper picks it up. What a way to live."

"Is she watched at home then?" asked Phil. "How many minders are in the house? Are you sure all this is worth it Jimmy? You will end up with your heart broke if you're not careful. These people are not like us. Money is their god. I am worried for you."

"Thanks, Phil, for watching out for me but I'll not be put off by her Dad and a couple of tough guys. There are ways and means if she loves me as much as I think she does," answered Jimmy.

"Finger's crossed eh Jimmy. Sorry I couldn't help overhearing your conversation." Tom sat down.

"That's ok boss. No secrets here," grinned Jimmy. "It's just that my love life has gone to the dogs, but I hope to get it back on track soon. Why did she have to have a rich Dad? If she had a Dad like you, boss, there wouldn't be a problem."

"Thanks for the back handed compliment Jimmy, but I may be rich myself one day and surprise you," laughed Tom.

"I didn't mean it like that," Jimmy apologized. "I know you have a good business and work hard. I'm just annoyed that her Dad would think me a fortune hunter without even knowing anything about me. I didn't know that Marianne had two halfpennies to rub together when I met her. She was special to me before I found out about her family. She never said anything."

Tom thought this a good opportunity to find out a bit more.

"What does her father do for a living?"

Jimmy answered.

"From what I have heard around their village, he started off as a haulage contractor, made his fortune, bought the offices in Chester and now has contracts in Canada and America. I don't know what he trades in but by the way he has accumulated money, it wouldn't surprise me if he was dodgy, maybe dealing drugs on the side. But that's just a guess. One person told me he has a heliport at the back of the property." Phil shook his head.

"I 'm worried about you, Jimmy, lad. I wish you had never met her. I have a bad feeling about all this and wish you would just forget all about her."

"Come on Phil let's get back to work. I'm a big lad now I have to make my own mind up," laughed Jimmy.

Whilst Tom was gleaning what information he could from Phil and Jimmy, Mike was busy surveying the comings and goings at Marianne's home.

"The father must be away on business," Mike informed Tom. "He was nowhere to be seen." They knew from Jimmy that Marianne's mother had died when she was little. There was a housekeeper in the house and two other employees, a gardener and a maintenance man but they were there to see no one got into the grounds. Minders, according to Jimmy.

"Marianne drives an M. G. sports car. How the other half live, eh Tom?" Mick had found out that she went out in the car a couple of times a week, but never on regular days. He followed her one day to the offices in Chester so he surmised she must be going to work there. He hadn't seen anyone else go in and out of the property except the postman, who called on the intercom and the gate opened to let him in. He had never seen a dog or heard one bark.

"Here's the plan Tom," Mick had informed him that week. "I don't want to waste any time on this job. It seems to be cut and dried. You organize a car by next Wednesday and hopefully the father won't be around. We can always double check if the helicopter is back. I can get over the wall if I stand on the bonnet of the car. It's not that high. The lane is quiet so we won't be seen. It won't take me long to get into the house. All you have to do is to wait outside for me. That's not too much to ask is it?" Tom stared at Mick.

"You are out of your mind. You are so greedy to get your hands-on money you are taking risks. You have not thought it through. How do you know they keep money in the house?" Tom had a bad feeling about the whole idea.

"Have you thought how you will get back over the wall? How do you know the whole place isn't alarmed? Is there money there for definite?"

"Oh, to hell with you Tom," replied Mick angrily. "You are always a ditherer. If I hadn't got you out of a mess in the first place, your precious wife and kids would be living in a tent by now. Get a grip and be a bit more positive. If you don't take risks in life you never get anywhere." Tom could see there was no changing Mick's mind.

"Ok," sighed Tom. "But let's not rush this. Let's go over it again properly for both our sakes." He now knew that Mick would take a gun with him and God knows what would happen if things started to go wrong. Finally, Mick began to see the sense in Tom's argument.

"We'll just find out from that lad of yours more about where they keep their cash. I'll wait another week and then we're doing it for sure."

Tom was at his wit's end wondering how to approach the subject with Jimmy when he had a stroke of luck. Jimmy had received a letter from Marianne. Luckily for him, the father was still away when the letter arrived and she had been keeping her eye out for the postman each morning before the housekeeper picked up the mail. She phoned Jimmy that evening.

Jimmy was beaming as he came in to work on the Friday morning.

"Guess what Phil," he shouted, "I've heard from Marianne. It's all on again. She's going to meet me next Tuesday evening. Her Dad is home for the weekend and then off again to Jersey on the Monday so the coast will be clear." Phil just nodded. He was worried for the lad. He had a gut feeling Jimmy was going to be let down badly and voiced his feelings as they sat down to their tea break later that morning.

Jimmy was still on a high.

"We can see each other every time her Dad goes away. I don't know how it will all pan out but I don't care. I love her Phil." Phil looked at his young workmate.

"I'm pleased for you Jimmy, honest, and hope you don't get let down. You're no gold digger. As you said, you didn't know she had money when you started going out together. Let's hope her father sees that." Jimmy said nothing. 'The money was just a bonus' he told himself. 'She is the one for me anyway'.

Tom was underneath a car fixing the exhaust that morning and had overheard all their conversation.

I suppose I will have to get hold of Mick and tell him we can find out for sure when the father is away on business. We need to find out where he keeps his cash before we make a move. God help me. If only I had not got involved with him in the first place. But I did and am paying the price now. I only hope I can start next year with a clean slate and that bloody brother -in-law of mine is safely on the other side of the world.

Tom managed to talk Mick into waiting till they could find out where the cash was kept. He made sure he listened in to Phil and Jimmy's conversations whenever Marianne's name was mentioned. One day he struck lucky.

"Guess what Phil," Jimmy began. "Marianne is planning to take me to Silverstone the week after next for the weekend. Her Dad is away in Germany for two weeks and she says she can spin the housekeeper a yarn. She wants to treat me to the Grand Prix. I have been on about it and told her I have always wanted to go but my wages won't stretch to that."

"Lucky you," answered Phil. "Wish now I had a woman to treat me to that. She must have pots of money."

"Well keep this to yourself Phil, but she let slip that her Dad has a safe in the house. She knows the combination and if she is a bit strapped for cash, she dips into it. He never checks. He trusts her. She has been doing that for a while."

"That's very dishonest," retorted Phil. "Money has no value to them obviously. Easy come, easy go I suppose."

Tom breathed a sigh of relief as he overheard all they were saying. At last, he could soon put this scheme of Mick's behind him.

Mick had been checking over the property with a fine-tooth comb. He now knew Marianne came home through the gates at five-thirty on the days she went out. There was no dog on the property. The wall was only five-foot-high and no glass or barbed wire on the top to deter a burglar. There were probably security lights but he would have to chance that. He would go on a light night and the lights wouldn't be noticed. He would be well able to reach the house without being noticed. Tom had the car all lined up. Everything was in place. He decided that nine o clock would be a good time as everyone would have eaten and be relaxing for the evening.

On the night they had decided upon, Tom drove slowly up the lane. No -one was around. Mick quickly scrambled on to the car bonnet and was up and over the wall in a flash. Tom drove off and was to come back in an hour as Mick had told him to.

Mick jumped down and lay on the ground for a minute. No-one was around. He noticed a ladder propped up against a shed and quickly moved it nearer the wall in case he had to make a quick getaway. He made his way around the side of the lawn and ducked behind a tree at the back of the house. He could hear a television in one of the downstairs rooms and someone laughing.

'So far, so good,' he breathed. He tried the back door. It was locked. He cursed under his breath. He skirted round the house until he came across the French doors. He carefully peered in. It was the dining room and everything had been cleared away.

He tried the handles. The doors were locked but the lock was not very secure. Mick had the forethought to carry a jemmy with him in case he needed it. Levering it between the lock and the door panel he was soon inside the dining room. He put on a black mask and looked around trying to get his bearings. He located where the television was and heard talking. There were at least two in that room, he thought to himself. My luck is holding. He put his hand in his pocket and put his hand over his gun. He hoped he would not have to use it. He listened outside the television room and heard men discussing the programme they were watching. 'I now know where the minders are,' he breathed. The housekeeper is probably in bed by now, he thought, hopefully. He made his way to the staircase.

There was no sound coming from the upstairs bedrooms. He supposed Marianne would be in one of these rooms but he was trusting a lot to luck. He listened outside the first bedroom. It was silent and the door slightly ajar. The next room was a bathroom. It was empty. Mick slowly made his way along the corridor until he came to a bedroom where the door was closed. He smelt perfume.

This is the room, he was certain. *This is her room.* He looked at his watch. It had taken half an hour up to now. He must keep an eye on the time. *Hope to God she is asleep. I'm taking a big chance here.* He took a deep breath, and opened the door slowly, gun in his hand. He sighed with relief as he saw Marianne was lying on the bed, with her eyes closed, earphones in, listening to music.

Quickly he moved to the side of the bed and clapped his hand over her mouth. She opened her eyes and tried to see who was there. What she saw terrified her. Her eyes were wide open in fright as she made out a dark figure with a mask on, holding a gun. She started to shake.

"Scream and I'll kill you," hissed Mike. She shook her head. He took his hand from her mouth slowly whilst holding the gun to her head.

"What do you want," Marianne managed to stammer.

"Not you if that's what you're thinking," growled Mick. "Get a dressing gown on and take me to the safe. You alert those monkeys downstairs and you're all dead. Do you get that?" He shook her violently. She nodded as she grabbed her dressing gown off the bed.

Tom heard the helicopter land and parked up in the lane. At the same moment Mick heard it too.

"God, what's this? Your old man is supposed to be in Germany. Quick," He gave her a shove. "Get downstairs and go out of the French windows." He grabbed her arm practically pushing her down the stairs. "Hurry up you bitch. Let's get out of here." He stuck the gun in her back as he hurried her across the lawn and grabbed the ladder. "Get over the wall," he whispered as he got hold of her ankle and pushed her upwards. Marianne scrambled up the ladder. Mick scrambled up after her. They jumped down the other side. Marianne lost her balance. Her legs felt like jelly. Sobbing, she struggled to get to her feet. She heard a car pull alongside with the engine running. Mick shoved her into the back seat and got in beside her.

"What the hell," Tom yelled. "What are you doing with her?"

"Just shut up and drive. Put your hood up and don't turn round. I need time to think of something," Mick turned to Marianne.

"You just better pray that your old man thinks you're worth sending back. That's all I can say." He poked the gun in her side as she cringed back in the seat and glared at him as he covered her eyes with an old cloth he had found in the back of the car.

As Tom was driving at top speed away from the house Mick checked that the cloth was still secure covering Marianne's eyes. The last thing he wanted was for her to be able to see him. He would have to kill her then.

"You keep bloody well quiet or I'll stuff somethin' in your gob," he growled at her. She had not stopped shaking and didn't utter a word.

"Take your next right," Mick instructed. "Then carry on till I tell you otherwise." Tom complied. His mind was in a blur. How would they get out of this one? After about two miles Mick told him to turn off up a lane. Tom knew this place. It was a caravan park closed up for the winter. Tom turned his lights off and drove slowly around the park. There were no lights on and no one around.

"Stop here," said Mick. Tom pulled up near a caravan tucked away in a corner. "This'll do for tonight, then we'll think of something," said Mick. "Get out," he snarled at Marianne, grabbing her arm tightly. She stumbled out of the car, her free arm wildly feeling for anything to grab to keep her balance. Mick forced the caravan door open with his jemmy and pushed her inside. She sprawled on to the floor and Mick slammed the door.

"What the hell are we going to do with her," spat out Tom. "You bloody idiot. We'll go down for this, for sure." Mick secured the caravan door and then they both sat in the car. Mick appeared calm.

"Now we failed to get any money from the house and we're landed with her. The only option left is to demand a ransom."

"Oh my God," said Tom. "It just gets worse and worse."

"Don't be such a wimp, Tom," snapped Mick. "We've landed a golden opportunity here. Her old man is a millionaire and we hold all the cards. He won't mind parting with a bit of cash to get his precious daughter back, you'll see."

Mick disappeared back into the caravan to check on Marianne. He spoke to her.

"I won't harm you if you do as I say. I'll get you some water before I go and bring you some food tomorrow. I'll have to tie you up. I don't trust you not to try and get away." He pushed her down on a seat and tied her arms and feet with a tow rope he had found in the boot of the car. He got a cup of water from the outside tap and held it while she drank.

"Now you keep quiet and I'll be back tomorrow. If your Dad coughs up you will be home soon." He slammed the door and she was left alone in the dark.

"She's not going anywhere," Mick informed Tom as he got back into the car. He gave a sigh of relief. "Let's just get back home and meet up tomorrow afternoon and we can plan what to do next. I can't think straight until I've had a bit of sleep." Tom couldn't speak. He was shocked to think Mick could leave this young girl trussed up in a caravan in the middle of the night and go home to sleep.

"Thank God she has not seen our faces. We must make sure of that." "We have to be careful not to let her hear our names as well. Just drive us back and get rid of that car as soon as poss. This will be ok as long as we are careful." Tom was not convinced. He drove back deep in thought. His primary worry at that precise moment was how to approach Cathie about where he had been all night. He knew she would be out of her mind with worry.

Cathie remembered that night vividly. She still felt sick in her stomach as she recalled the horror of it all.

Earlier that day Tom had told her that he was taking Mrs. Thomas to the airport for one of her holiday breaks to Spain. Cathie thought nothing of it. Mrs. Thomas was a valued customer.

"Bye, darling. Drive carefully. Love you," were her parting words to him that evening as she settled down with the children in front of the television.

"Bye, love you all," Tom called as he went through the door. She recalled that moment as the final trust and happiness she would know. The end of a marriage.

She went to bed around ten-thirty after she had listened to the news. She checked the children. All were sleeping soundly. She read for a while and then drifted off to sleep. Something awoke her during the night and she sat up with a start. Instinctively she felt Tom's side of the bed, then looked at the clock. The bed was empty. "Four o clock," she muttered to herself. "He should have been home hours ago. He must have broken down. Why hasn't he phoned?" Her stomach started to churn over. "I hope he has not been in an accident." She shook herself. "Don't be so morbid Cathie. The police would come and tell me if it was bad news." She crept downstairs and quietly made herself a cup of tea. Another hour went by and still no sign of Tom.

If he's not home by six, I'm going to ring the hospital. She was frantic with worry. *He would have contacted me somehow if he could.* Six o clock came round and still no Tom. She picked up the phone and dialed the accident and emergency unit of the general hospital.

"No-one here under that name has been admitted overnight," the voice on the other end of the phone informed her. She breathed easier. *He was not dead or the police would have been around before now. Where was he?* Cathie was puzzled. She decided to ring Jenny. Surprised to hear from her sister so early in the morning, Jenny knew immediately that something was wrong.

"It's Tom, he's not come home," Cathie informed her, "He hasn't been home all night. He's not been in an accident, I've checked. I don't know what has happened to him."

"How strange," replied Jenny. "I'm sure he will turn up soon with a good explanation. His car could have broken down miles from a phone box." She tried to reassure her sister. "He's a home bird. He's not like Mick. He's not here either but he stays away a lot of the time anyway thank goodness. That gives the girls and I a bit of peace. He's like an old tomcat always prowling about at night. Unlike you, I'm glad to see the back of him. But Cathie, seriously, if Tom's not back by the time I've dropped the girls off at school I'll come over."

"Thanks Jenny, let's hope I have some news before then. I'll keep you posted." As she was talking on the phone, she heard his car draw up outside. "Oh, thank God Jenny, he's home. I'll ring you later." She put the phone down and hurried to the door. Tom came in and gave her a hug. "Wherever have you been, Tom?" she questioned him. "I've been out of my mind with worry."

Tom sat down at the kitchen table.

"Are the kids still asleep?" he asked her. She nodded and sat opposite him. "I'm in a heap of bother Cathie. I don't know what to do and I can't tell you just yet." She stared at him. He was as white as a ghost.

"Have you been in an accident, Tom?" she enquired tentatively. "You haven't run anyone over, have you?"

"No Cathie, it's nothing like that. I'm just a bit shook up that's all. Get us a cup of tea will you love? I'll be alright in a bit. I must go into work. I will tell you, but please be patient for a while. It's complicated." Tom needed to think. He needed to get the story straight with Mick. They needed to work out what the hell they were going to do with that girl.

Chapter Nineteen

Jimmy came bursting into work the next morning and made a beeline for Phil.

"You'll never guess what's happened Phil," he began. Phil looked up from under the bonnet of the car he was working on. "Marianne's been kidnapped. It's all over the news."

"My God," said Phil, "that's awful. Hope she's not been harmed. Do the police have any clue?"

"There's nothing except that she's been kidnapped. I expect the police are being cautious in case it puts her in danger. There's nothing I can do to help her Phil. I do love her. I can't think straight. She must be terrified."

Jimmy was near to tears.

"Calm down lad. Let's wait till Tom gets in and maybe he will let you have the day off. You're as white as a sheet."

"I feel sick, to be honest Phil. It's 'cos her Dad's got money obviously. They must mean to ransom her. Her family must be in bits." At that moment Tom walked in and overheard them. He looked surprised.

"What's this Jimmy? Is this to do with the girl you have been seeing?"

"The girl's been kidnapped, Tom," said Phil. "The lad's very upset. Do you think he could have the day off to sort himself out?"

"Without question," answered Tom looking very concerned. He put his hand on Jimmy's shoulder. "You must be out of your mind with worry, Jimmy lad. Go and see what you can find out and if you feel up to it come back and let us know later. I'll fill in for you today."

"Thanks ever so much boss. I'll make up the time. See you both later."

Tom's head was buzzing but he had to make sure he played the innocent in front of Phil.

"I wonder who'd do a thing like that Phil?" he questioned. "Fancy something like that happening around here. You said you suspected the girl's father to be involved with drug-running. I expect it's something to do with that. They'll stop at nothing if someone upsets them."

"I think you're right, Tom," agreed Phil. "Let's pray no harm comes to the lass. She must be frightened to death. The police around here won't know what has hit them. A stolen bike or a parking fine is all the action they've had to deal with in a while. They never got to the bottom of those garage break-ins we had. They've given up on those by now I suppose. Makes you wonder what they do all day in this area. I expect the Chester police are calling the shots with this one. Kidnapping is a very serious offence."

Tom was glad when Phil had finished talking. What he said about the seriousness of the crime made his stomach turn over. He had to keep his nerve.

"You're probably right Phil. Let's hope Jimmy has some better news when he gets back."

Jimmy called in at the garage later that afternoon. He looked quite ill.

"There's been no word about her whereabouts Phil," he told him. "And no word from the kidnappers yet. She must be cold and hungry and stuffed down a drain for all we know. She may even be dead by now." He put his head down and started to sob. Phil walked over to him and lifted his head up.

"Come on now. None of that talk. You have to think positive. Have you seen any of the family?" Jimmy sniffed and shook his head.

"I don't know anyone at the house. I do know what her Dad looks like though. I was on my way into the police station when he came barging out. He doesn't know me. He was shouting and swearing. His face was like thunder. I just kept out of the way 'till he got in his car. Then I told the police who I was and asked if there was any news. They wouldn't tell me anythin' so I'm none the wiser now. I feel terrible. I can only talk to you about it Phil. I don't know what to do next."

"You can't do anything Jimmy lad, only wait and pray if you've a mind to. I'm here for you if you need me."

"Thanks a lot Phil," answered Jimmy.

Tom was watching and listening to all of this from the back of the garage as he was working out how to get rid of the getaway car as soon as possible. It would have all their fingerprints all over it.

What a bloody awful mess. I only hope Mick keeps his cool if she tries to get away. I really don't trust him not to use that gun.

Tom told Phil he had an appointment with the bank manager and slipped off to meet Mick. They had arranged to meet in town at a cafe at three o clock. They ordered coffee.

"Are you quite sure you want to go ahead and demand a ransom Mick?" pleaded Tom. "Can't we just dump her somewhere and then anonymously phone the police to tell them where she is? No-one would get hurt and no-one would be any the wiser." Mick laughed.

"Are you mad? You don't honestly think we have gone through all this for nothing. Come on Tom, don't be stupid all your life. We are sitting on a fortune here."

"I don't like the 'we' in all this Mick," protested Tom. "I don't want any part of it. It's too risky."

"Don't start all that rubbish again Tom. I'm sick of hearing it. You are involved whether you like it or not. You can't back out. You helped me kidnap her, didn't you? You're in it as deep as I am and don't you ever forget it."

"For Christ's sake Mick, when will you ever stop?"

"When I have the money Tom, simple as that." Tom was exasperated. There was no reasoning with Mick. He had gone beyond thinking straight. All he could see was money.

"Let's get on with it and plan our next move," said Mick impatiently. "We're just wasting time. We have to deal with the change of plan and make the best of a bad situation. We have a young girl hold up and blindfolded and trussed up in a caravan. We have to do something. Do you think the place is safe enough or shall we move her somewhere else?" Tom hesitated.

"Well, I suppose it's as good as anywhere. I can't think of anywhere better off hand. But we will have to take her some food and a drink as soon as it goes dark. She will be terrified wondering if she's going to die out there if we don't come back."

"I told her I would be back," Mick answered gruffly. "She understands we want ransom money so why would we harm her? I have been thinking. As soon as it's dark we'll drive over there as you said and take her some food. We'll take her to the telephone box on the camp. She can let her Dad know she is still alive and tell him to get us forty grand together in used notes by tomorrow. Then she will ring him again at the same time. Do you think that's a plan?"

"I suppose it is," agreed Tom reluctantly. We'll have to decide where he's to drop the money off."

"That's the tricky bit," agreed Mick. "I need to sleep on that one. Come on, it's getting dark. Let's get over there and sort her out.

Marianne lay on the seat of the caravan. She was cold and frightened. Her wrists and ankles were raw with trying to wriggle out of the rope ties. She felt so degraded. She had needed the toilet so bad she had to shuffle to the edge of the bench and just wet herself. She shuffled back and started to cry again.

"What if they don't come back?' she whimpered to herself. "I will starve to death and it maybe next spring before I was found. Oh God, if you are up there please help me?" she begged. Hour after hour dragged by. She heard birds singing so she knew it was daylight. She felt a bit better. "Just be strong," she told herself firmly. "He promised to come back. He would have killed me last night if he'd a mind too. He wants ransom money." She took a deep breath. "Just be brave and keep that thought in your head," she told herself firmly. She shouted loudly in case anyone was about. Nobody answered. No one was around the camp at that time of year. She kept trying to wriggle till her wrists were even more painful but the rope held firm.

She waited for what seemed a lifetime straining her ears for the sound of a car engine. She was cold, wet and hungry. Totally dejected and miserable. At long last she heard the sound of a car approaching. It stopped outside the caravan. She heard voices.

"Here, I've brought you something to eat. I said I would." She heard the same voice who had taken her from her bedroom. He untied her wrists. She winced at the pain. Tears rolled down her cheeks.

"Well, you shouldn't have tried to escape, should you?" said the voice unsympathetically. "Eat your food." He shoved a sandwich into her hand. She tried to hold on to it. She was starving. "Hold it tighter, stupid. We haven't got all night." The feeling started to come back into her fingers and painfully she gripped the sandwich and started to eat. When she had finished, he held a bottle to her mouth. "Here, drink this and when you are done you can put this old coat on and we are going to phone your old fella."

Marianne felt for the sleeves of the coat and gratefully wrapped it around her. She had never in her life felt as cold as she did now.

"Come on, we need to go." Mick grabbed her arm and she felt her way to the door and down the steps. He led her along a path and after a few minutes he stopped. "Right, tell me your phone number and you can speak to your old man. Just say hello so he can hear your voice. That's all you say, do you understand?" He hissed menacingly and shook her.

"Yes, yes," she nodded. She told him the number and he dialed and put money in the box when he heard someone pick up the phone at the other end. He shoved the phone into Marianne's hand. She heard her father answer the phone.

"Hello Dad," she said shakily.

"Thank God," her father sounded so relieved. "Where are you? Are you all right?" Mick snatched the phone from her. He spoke through his scarf to muffle his voice.

"If you want to see your daughter again you do as I say," he began. Silence at the other end of the phone. "You contact the police and she's a goner. You understand?"

"I can do without the police interfering," came back the reply. "I presume you want money?"

"You're right there," answered Mick, "I want forty grand. You won't even miss that from what I've seen of your place. Used notes mind."

"Just keep my girl safe," answered Charlie Maxwell. "I can get you the money by tomorrow. I just want my girl back unharmed."

"Well, just do as I say then," answered Mick, putting more money in the box. "The way I see it is this. You get the forty grand in used notes by this time tomorrow and you'll get your precious daughter back. Any funny business and you'll never see her again. Is that clear?"

"As crystal," replied Maxwell. "Where shall I meet you?" Mick told him he would ring the next day at the same time to arrange the exchange. Then he hung up.

Marianne had overheard the conversation and her heart sank. She would have to spend another twenty-four hours cold, blindfolded, and tied up in the caravan.

As they drove away from the campsite Mick and Tom fell silent. Each of them was racking their brains for a solution to the mess they had got themselves into. At last Tom spoke.

"I think I have a plan," he said. Mick looked across at him hopefully. "It will have to be a bloody good one," he remarked.

"The way I see it is this," Tom began. "When we phone Maxwell again, we will tell him to drive to Chester alone. I'm sure he hasn't told the police about the ransom demand. They would start delving into his business."

"Yes, go on," said Mick impatiently. Tom continued.

"We 'll tell him to leave the money in a cafe on the other side of town. We'll collect it when we have checked he came on his own, go back for the girl and drop her off somewhere near his house. He has to trust us and I think he will play ball."

"Well, I can't think of anything better," admitted Mick. "Ok, we'll do it your way." They drove home discussing and going over their plans. The next day Mick drove over to Chester and made a note of the phone box numbers they planned to use.

The next evening after telling Cathie he was taking a customer to the airport Tom made his escape and headed over to get Mick out of the pub. They had decided to take the truck and the car this time. They headed for the caravan site, gave Marianne something to eat and drink and took her back to the phone box. Mick rang the number and it was answered straight away.

"I've got your filthy money," Mick heard Charlie Maxwell on the other end of the phone. "When do I get my daughter back?"

"Hope you haven't told anyone else or you won't see her

again. I did warn you, understood?" Mick answered, his voice disguised by his scarf. "Listen careful- Get to the phone box by the cathedral at eight o clock tomorrow morning. I'll call you there and tell you where to take the money."

"This is a bloody wild goose chase," shouted Maxwell down the phone. "Just hand her over. Money means nothing to me. You know I don't have nothing to do with the police. Now let me speak to my daughter." Mick shoved the phone to Marianne's ear.

"I am ok Dad. Just do as he says." she whimpered. Mick snatched the phone back. "Just making sure," Mick replied calmly. Don't try any funny business with that heavy mob of yours. Just do as I say." He rang off. He and Tom sat in their vehicles and waited for morning.

Mick parked up near the phone box around the corner from the cathedral.

Charlie Maxwell was at the allotted phone box at a quarter to eight. After about twenty minutes the phone rang.

"Go to the Rainbow cafe on Gloucester Street and put the money behind the toilet in the second cubicle then go back to this phone box and I will tell you where and when to pick up your daughter. I will keep my word if you do exactly as I say. I didn't want to take her in the first place. She just got in the way. I have not harmed her but make no mistake. If you cross me you will never see her again."

"Yes, I've heard all that yesterday," replied Maxwell, anxious to get off the phone. "Let's just get this over with."

Tom was waiting over the road from the Rainbow cafe. He saw Maxwell draw up and enter the cafe with a bag under his arm. Tom went inside and ordered a coffee. Maxwell went straight to the gent's toilets and when he came out the bag was gone. He watched as Maxwell got into his car and drove off. Then he went straight to the toilet cubicle and retrieved the bag. He went back to his car and checked the contents. There was a large number of used notes in the bag, presumably what they had asked for. He rang Mick at the phone box where he was waiting and confirmed that they had the money.

"I'll wait here till I've spoken again to Maxwell and made sure he is on his own. You bring the girl and ditch her as we arranged and then I believe we are home and dry." Mick told him. "And don't forget to hide the money where I told you and dump the hold all.

"Yes, I think we will be ok, thank God, and I will do as you say with the money. Tom sounded relieved. This is going well for once Tom thought to himself as he drove back to the caravan site to get Marianne. He had the shock of his life when he got there. He quickly reversed the car around a corner out of sight, got out and peered around the back of a nearby van. There were police cars and an ambulance parked outside the caravan. Marianne was walking shakily towards the ambulance supported by a paramedic. Tom quickly got back into his car and made his way off the site.

'Oh my God', thought Tom to himself.' Mick will have told Maxwell by now where we had intended to drop her off. Maxwell will think we have double crossed him and done a runner. He'll hound us down. However, did she manage to escape? We're done for now that's for sure.' He glanced in his mirror and to his horror he saw the blue light of the police car following behind.

Chapter Twenty

A few hours previous Marianne had finally wriggled her hands free from the ropes. Her skin was raw and bleeding, but she didn't feel anything. Her only thought was to get to the phone box. She managed to untie her feet and take off the blindfold. Panicking in case the men came back before she could raise the alarm, she stumbled across to the phone box hoping against hope not to see the headlights of a car. Her luck held. She had no money and quickly dialled 999.

"Tell me where you are love," a friendly voice enquired as she gabbled out her story.

"I've no idea," cried Marianne. "Please hurry."

"Just describe anything you can see around you," persisted the person on the other end of the phone.

"I 've heard a clock chiming and I can hear a river nearby. It's just caravans everywhere."

"Oh, I know where you are," the voice sounded relieved. "Just wait there and I'll get police and an ambulance out to you straight away and stay hidden if you hear anyone about. They won't be long."

Marianne paced up and down around the telephone box until at last she heard a siren in the distance, then saw two police cars and an ambulance pull up. She burst into tears with relief.

"We'll take you to the hospital love, for a checkup. We'll put dressings on your wrists on the way." The medic put his arms around her.

"Just point out which van you were held in before we go. We can get a statement later when you are in the hospital," one of the policemen told her. She nodded and got into the back of the ambulance.

The police heard Tom's car starting off and two of them jumped in the police car to follow, leaving the other police to cordon off the van for evidence. Tom spotted the police car in his mirror and put his foot down. He was pouring with sweat and trying to concentrate on the road and not panic. He could not get rid of the sound of the police siren. He knew the roads like the back of his hand. After about two miles of careering down the main road Tom suddenly made a sharp right. He knew this backroad and was convinced he could lose the police car. He twisted and turned and gripped the steering wheel tightly to keep the car on the narrow lanes. After what seemed like a lifetime, he had not managed to shake them off and had nearly overturned the car twice. He was desperate now especially when he glanced down at the petrol gauge. He shot round the next bend and decided to dump the car and make a run for it. The petrol gauge was on empty. He shot out of the car and ran towards the woods. The police were still on his tail. They saw where he was heading and gave chase on foot. Tom was not as fit as the police and they were soon gaining on him. They caught up with him quite quickly and threw him to the ground and handcuffed him. Tom would never forget the next few minutes. He was immediately put under arrest for failing to stop his vehicle and for dangerous driving. He was told his rights.

This is it. If they find the money I'm done for. My life will be ruined, and all through that bloody Mick and his greed'

Unaware that anything was wrong, Mick had phoned Maxwell and told him they would drop the girl off near the bus station later that morning and he was to wait in the waiting room. Mick waited and waited but the girl did not appear. Maxwell was pacing up and down in the waiting room looking all around for the appearance of his daughter. By twelve o clock they each came to the conclusion that something was wrong. Mick was puzzled. What had happened to Tom and the girl and more importantly what had happened to the money. He set off in his truck back to the campsite.

Maxwell had no alternative. He went straight to the police station. He was sure he had been double-crossed. He was devastated and convinced his daughter was dead. He was shocked and relieved to hear that Marianne had managed to escape and was now safe and well in hospital.

"Thank the Lord," he muttered and made a vow there and then to himself that he would give up his drug dealing from then on and lead a better life.

"I'll get over to the hospital straight away," he told the police.

"We will need a statement as soon as you have seen your daughter," the desk sergeant told him.

"Oh, by the way," said Maxwell. "Can you check the Rainbow cafe. I put five grand in used notes in the second toilet cubicle this morning. I expect it's gone but worth a check." He was not going to tell the police he had forty grand of undeclared used notes at his disposal.

The desk sergeant looked at him.

"I'll send someone over there straight away, sir, but I suspect it was picked up as they would have been watching you drop it off. "

Mick was bewildered. The camp site was deserted. He drove back to Tom's garage. What on earth had happened? He desperately needed to find Tom. He found Phil.

"Have you seen Tom," he enquired. "I need to get hold of him. It's urgent."

"Sorry Mick. I haven't seen him. You ok? What's so urgent?"

"We were supposed to meet up. I had a bit of business for him. I hope he's not been in an accident.

Phil answered.

"I'm sure we would have heard if he had been in an accident. Maybe he forgot he was meeting you." Mick tried another line of questioning.

"Not to worry. You are right and if Tom doesn't want the business I'm not going to bother again. See you Phil. Oh, by the way." Mick changed tactics. "Is that lad of yours in? It's big news this kidnapping. Has he heard anything?"

"He's so upset Mick. I can't get him to concentrate on anything. I've given him the day off," Phil replied.

"Oh, I expect we'll hear something soon. Bye Phil."

Mick was worried sick. He drove over to find Norma.

"Hello," she sounded surprised. "What are you doing here?"

"Shut up and listen," Mick told her. "Don't go blabbing your mouth off to anyone," he warned her. "We've got the money to get to Oz. Just that I have to catch up with Tom. He has it and I can't find him. If he has double crossed me, I swear I'll kill him. We could be gone by next week. We have our visas and everything. I just need to find him." Norma clapped her hands together.

"Oh, Mick at last. Tom wouldn't cross you. I'm certain of it. You must trust him. "

"I bloody well hope he wouldn't. I don't trust anyone. Have you got the money I gave you safe?"

"Of course, it's safe at home. No one knows it's there."

"Good girl," replied Mick. "I'll carry on looking for Tom and I'll come back as soon as I've found him. Do the rest of your packing."

"No more to do Mick. I've been packed for months." She gave him a kiss and a hug. He muttered goodbye and sat outside in his truck.

"Where the hell would he have gone?" He headed off towards Tom's house.

Cathie was sitting clutching a mug of tea when she heard the doorbell ring.

"Thank the Lord," she said to herself. "Tom's home safe at last. He must have forgotten his key. I hope he will tell me now what is wrong." She muttered this to herself as she hurried to open the door. She was surprised and disappointed to see her brother-in-law on the doorstep.

"Mick," she said, startled. "What are you doing here? Where's Tom?"

"Now, I thought you could tell me that," answered Mick. "I've been looking for him all morning." Cathie was really worried.

"He hasn't been home all night. The night before he came

back late and he was as white as a sheet. He wouldn't tell me what was wrong and promised to tell me last night, but he never came home. I don't know what's going on but he must be in some sort of serious trouble. Maybe he's witnessed some crime and they are after him?" She looked at Mick for conformation but his face was blank.

"I wish I could throw some light on the matter Cathie." His voice full of concern. "I'll carry on looking for him and phone you if I have any news."

"Thanks Mick," replied Cathie gratefully.

As Cathie waited anxiously, later that morning the phone rang. It was Tom.

"Cathie, I'm so very sorry. I've ruined everything." Cathie cut in.

"Where are you Tom? Are you hurt? What has happened?" Tom answered.

"I'm at the police station in Chester. I've been arrested." Cathie put her hand over her mouth to stop herself from crying out.

"Why Tom, for what? What have you done?"

"It's serious Cathie darling. I'm so sorry. They won't let me out. I don't think they will even let me see you. Get our solicitor for me, will you?"

"Oh Tom, surely it can't be that bad, but I'll get the solicitor to come over as soon as I can. Don't worry darling. He'll soon straighten this out. It must be a mistake. Be strong. Me and the kids love you."

"Love you all too Cathie." Tom began to sob. "I'm so sorry

Cathie." He hung up.

Mick went back to the garage to find out if anyone had heard anything. Jimmy was there chatting excitedly to Phil.

"It's been on the news Phil. She's back home safe and not a hair on her head has been harmed. What a miracle. Apparently, the kidnapping went wrong and she managed to escape. The bloke what took her has been caught. The police have him now. She must have been so frightened Phil. Thank God she managed to escape. They could have murdered her."

Mick overheard the conversation and went cold. He was shocked. So, they had Tom in custody. Well, more fool him for letting his self get caught. His first thoughts were, what had happened to the money. Had Tom managed to pick it up and hide it from the cops.

"Hi, lads, I overheard your good news Jimmy. Do they know who the fella is who took her? I wonder if he's from around here? We may know him."

"They've not said anything on the news, Mick," answered Phil.

"Not to worry, we'll hear soon enough," said Mick calmly. I just came in to see if Tom was back. I'll catch up with him tomorrow. See you both."

Mick had no intention of going home yet. He drove straight to the cafe to see if the money was still there. He ordered a coffee and went to the gents. He felt around the back of the toilet. Nothing. He cursed 'The police must have It,' he thought to himself. 'I only hope Tom had the gumption to hide it before he was caught. I never have any bloody luck.'

Slowly it dawned on Mick that no one suspected he was involved. They had got away with the previous robberies and although he had no further money from the last heist he was in the clear. All the blame for the kidnapping was falling on Tom.

Well, let's see how long you can keep your mouth shut, Tom. He was not too convinced. After all he had blackmailed Tom into doing the robberies with him. Tom was not going to take the wrap for this one. Mick realized that. He had to get away before Tom spilled everything he knew to the police. He had to move quickly.

Mick knew that Tom would squeal to the police that he had been blackmailed into providing the getaway car. They would know from Marianne that there was another man involved. Although she wouldn't be able to describe him, she could tell them that the man had a gun. Tom would name him for sure. What was it the law called it? Information in assisting them with their enquiries. That would help him get a lesser sentence if he co-operated, and the blackmail would be taken into account as mitigating circumstances. He would have no loyalty to a brother-in-law who was violent to his wife's sister and a blackmailer to boot.

He had a plan. He had only given Norma about a third of the money stash. He trusted no one. The remainder was in the barn on the smallholding. He headed in that direction. He assumed that Tom would inform the police of his plan to get to Australia. They would soon be watching the airports. He could no longer figure Norma in his plans. She would just be extra baggage and would slow him down. Let her meet some other mug to take her to Australia. He didn't need her and she wouldn't open her mouth. She would probably think he would come back for her.

He collected the money, his passport and a few clothes. Jenny, nor the children were anywhere to be seen.

"Off over at her fancy mans' for tea I shouldn't wonder," he muttered to himself. "Good luck to them and good riddance." He got into the truck and headed south to Newhaven port. He would get the ferry over to France that night. He didn't think the police would be checking that area yet.

He showed his passport and boarded the boat to Dieppe without any trouble. No sign of a police check. He breathed in the sea air and grinned to himself. 'So far so good. I've got plenty of money to see me through for a while', he thought to himself. He ordered a pint of beer and sat down and relaxed for the crossing. He didn't regret leaving England behind. Norma meant little to him, his wife and family even less. He planned to make a new start, maybe in the south of France. He would enjoy himself for a while, then get a truck driving job. He had it all worked out. No ties, no worries. 'I may meet a nice little French lass', he thought to himself. Life looked very promising.

Chapter Twenty-One

Tom looked round the police cell as he heard the cell door shut. He sat down on the bed and put his head in his hands. The police had told him to get some rest and he would be interviewed in the morning. He spent the night staring at the wall and hoping the police would not find the money. He would deny any knowledge of the kidnapping.

The next morning Tom sat nervously across the table where two officers sat and started to ask questions.

"Why were you on the caravan site? Why didn't you stop? Why did you lead us on a wild goose chase? Do you know anything about a girl being held in one of the caravans? If you do know anything it will go in your favour if you tell us what you know. Anyone else involved? Who is it?" They kept firing questions at him and Tom looked blank and bewildered.

The police continued.

"The girl told us there were two men, one with a gun. We will search your car and if we find a gun you could be looking at twenty years behind bars. So, if you know anything, now is the time to make a statement." Tom looked at the duty solicitor.

"No comment." He had made up his mind not to say anything until his own solicitor was present and hopefully the police would not find anything in the car. As long as he didn't admit to anything, they didn't have much to connect him to the kidnapping.

Cathie made arrangements to meet the solicitor. Jenny and the girls were staying with her for the day for moral support. She was heartbroken.

"Me and Jimmy will see to the garage for you," volunteered Phil. "Tom has always been a good boss. There must be an explanation. It must be a mistake. The police have obviously got the wrong man." Cathie didn't know what to think. She could not concentrate and burst into tears whenever she recalled Tom's phone call.

"Come on Cathie," her sister had told her. "Try and keep it together. You've got the children to think of. It's hard for them too."

Cathie blew her nose. "Thanks, Phil. At least the garage will be one less worry at the moment."

The police had taken Tom's car for fingerprinting and to search for the missing money. They were convinced they were on the right track; otherwise, why would Tom be cruising around near the caravan where Marianne had been tied up. They dusted the car for fingerprints and found a match for Marianne's on the back seat. They could not find any money and presumed Tom had hidden it before he reached the camp site.

"Let's give it one more search," said Detective Inspector Evans, the officer in charge. "When I worked with the drug squad, one of the places where they stashed the bags of powder we found in cars, was in the panels of the doors. They only clip into place and it would not take long to take the door panels off and put them back again. This guy owns a garage. He would be able to do that no problem.

The officers went back to the car and found that D.I. Evans had been quite right. They soon found the forty thousand pounds in used notes.

"Maxwell only told us he had parted with five grand. He's got some explaining to do as well. The taxman needs to know about this little lot."

Mr. Daniel Edwards had been Tom and Cathie's solicitor for years. He had dealt with buying their house and their business. He was a short stocky man, always in a pin striped suit. Tom swore he went to bed in it or at least wore pin striped pyjamas. He had an abrupt manner, but was always straight with them, and Cathie needed and trusted him now more than ever. As she sat across the desk in his office, he gave a sigh and shook his head.

"I cannot break this gently to you, Cathie," he began. "I've been to see Tom. It's not looking very good. Tom will be looking at a custodial sentence with all the evidence against him." Cathie put her hand to her mouth and tried to stop from breaking down in front of him.

"Why, Daniel? Whatever has made him go off the rails like this? What has he done that is so bad?" The solicitor shook his head.

"He won't tell me all of it Cathie. He kept saying over and over that he will tell you everything when he sees you. He is so ashamed and has been putting off facing you, but I insisted he had to see you. I have arranged a visiting order for next week. I hope he keeps his word and explains himself for all this trouble he has brought on your family." He hesitated. "At the moment he is being charged with failing to stop when required to do so, dangerous driving, conspiracy in an attempted armed robbery, and of taking a hostage. He is looking at fourteen years minimum I'm afraid." Cathie put her head in her hands, then looked over at Daniel. She was visibly shaking.

"My God. It's Tom who took that girl Jimmy knows isn't it?" He nodded. "I don't understand. How is he mixed up in that? My poor kids. How am I going to explain to them? I'll never forgive him for this. He can hurt me all he likes but he has involved the children. All their school friends will get to know what he has done. He's ruined our lives. The business will have to go. We will lose the house. I can't deal with all this. I hope I never have to see Tom again." She burst into floods of tears.

Daniel got up from behind his desk and put his arm around her.

"Come, come Cathie. Let's take this a step at a time. We have to deal with this. You are strong. You are a professional woman. You are just in shock at the moment. Your whole world has imploded. It may look as if you have no future without Tom but you will get on your feet again. You will do it for your children." Cathie blew her nose.

"Thank you, Daniel. You are right. My kids are the most important thing to me now. I have to stay strong for them."

"That's the spirit Cathie. Now let's confirm that visit for next week. You deserve an explanation. I will drive you to the remand centre and bring you home."

Tuesday came around. Cathie was dreading going to see Tom in the remand centre. She had never been inside a prison before. She had left the children with Jenny. She still had to face that problem. She had told them their father had to go away on business for a few days.

"Hello Cathie," said Tom quietly. They were sat in a room with a small table between them amongst other prisoners and their wives. He was wearing an orange leotard over his pullover.

She shuddered as she looked at him.

"I'm so very sorry Cathie," he began. "I don't know what else to say."

"You're sorry," Cathie's tone was bitter. "You can never be sorry enough for what you have done to our family. What puzzles me is why. Why did you break the law like that? I don't get it. You've ruined everything we have worked so hard for. You must have gone mad." Tom held his head in his hands and muttered.

"It was Mick, Cathie. He needed money to get out of his marriage and he had a hold over me. He was blackmailing me." Cathie stared at him.

"What do you mean, a hold over you? Why was he blackmailing you?"

"I did something ages ago when we first had the business, that I came to regret, and I was ashamed. If I had told you, you would probably have left me and taken the children. I couldn't risk that. But it doesn't matter now. You will take the kids away after I go down. I would want you to."

"That tells me nothing Tom. I want to know. I deserve to know."

Tom looked around and lowered his voice.

"I haven't told the police everything. They only know of the kidnapping job," he whispered.

"You mean there is more?" Cathie was astonished. Tom carried on in a low voice. "I hope I can trust you not to tell the police anything else I tell you."

"What you have been charged with is bad enough. You are

looking at fourteen years, Daniel says. I still don't understand how you got involved. I am waiting for an explanation."

Tom took a deep breath and started to confess to her in whispered tones about when it had all started.

"I had an affair Cathie. It was years ago. We were quarreling a lot at the time if you think back. The bills were piling up. I couldn't face listening to you going on about it and used to down the pub."

"Oh, it's all my fault is it?" Cathie spat back at him. "And who was this tart, this home wrecker. Do I know her? Was she worth all this?"

Tom started to speak again. He wanted to tell her everything now he had got started.

"It was Megan. I'm so sorry Cathie. She just threw herself at me, she wouldn't leave me alone. It's just a game to her and I kept trying to get rid of her and after a few months she found someone else."

"So, you and Megan had a cosy little affair for a few months while I was tucked up at home looking after your children. Wonderful."

"I knew you would hate me if you found out," replied Tom. "At the same time as this was going on, Mick was getting desperate to end his marriage. He needed money as he and Norma had planned to go to Australia. It was when he realized I was having an affair that he blackmailed me into getting getaway cars for the robberies he had planned.

"Norma set us up for the robbery at the Post Office where she works but the police haven't a clue about that one. Norma will keep her mouth shut if he leaves her some money. There were a couple more. I tried not to get involved but Mick had this hold over me." Tom decided he would confess the details of the other robberies at a later date.

Cathie was stunned. All this time she had believed and trusted that Tom was out at night working and earning money and all the time he was doing robberies with Mick and filtering the money back into the business. She stared hard at Tom then spoke.

"You're unbelievable. It's like a nightmare. That little tramp Megan can have you. I always knew there was something I hated about her. Now I know. I'll never forgive you for all this Tom. You are a cheat and a liar. You don't deserve me and the kids. I never want to see you again." With eyes full of tears, she got up and left.

Chapter Twenty-Two

Mick stepped off the boat and looked around. He felt as if a burden had been lifted off his shoulders.

"Free at last," he grinned, and looked around for the exit. He had no luggage, only the clothes he was wearing. Before he left the port, he changed up his money into francs, then hailed a cab. Luckily, the cab driver understood a smattering of English. Mick headed for the centre of town. He needed some clothes and essentials. He spent a while wandering around the shops, purchasing what he needed and then hailed another cab. He made the cabbie understand that he needed somewhere to stay. He was driven to a hotel but Mick shook his head. He needed a bed and breakfast establishment and not too expensive. He needed to make his money last. At last, the cab driver understood.

"Ah oui, chambre d'hotes," he nodded and drove up a side street with three-storey terraced houses on either side.

"Anywhere here will do," Mick pointed to a house and got his money out.

Mick picked a house that looked clean and he liked the name, La Belle Chateau. He knocked on the door and a middle-aged man answered.

"Do you speak English?" was the first thing Mick asked,

"Oui, yes I do," replied the man in a heavy French accent. "Do you need a room?"

"Yes, for a week or so. How much?" They discussed terms

and Mick seemed satisfied. He introduced himself as Will Johnson.

"Call me Will," he said.

"Claude," replied the Frenchman. "Come, I'll show you to your room. Breakfast is between eight and ten."

"Thanks, pal," replied Mick and counted out a week's money for his stay. "I'll settle myself in and then I need to eat." Claude led him up two flights of stairs, recommended a couple of local restaurants and then left Mick to settle in. Mick looked around the room. It was clean and basic with a wardrobe, desk and a chair, and a wash basin in the corner. He then tested the bed. "Yes, this will do me fine for a couple of weeks then I'll move on." He looked out of the window over the roof tops of the town. *No-one will think to trace me here. Yes, I think I will relax for a while before I get something to eat.* He stretched out on the bed and closed his eyes.

The next morning Claude was busy attending to his guests. It was a crisp frosty morning and he wrapped up warm and headed for the patisserie.

"Bonjour, Madame," he greeted the woman behind the counter. He ordered fresh croissants, pastries and rolls then hurried back to his guest house to set out the breakfast. This was Claude's daily routine. He had several guests booked in at the moment and business was good.

Mick decided not to have breakfast the next morning, but to go straight out and find out the train times and the money he would need to travel further south. He had planned to stay a while at this comfortable bed and breakfast hotel but something told him he must not get complacent.

Things are going my way for once. I'm not used to this. It feels strange.

The following morning, Claude made his usual trip to the patisserie. As he was setting out the breakfasts it was his habit to put on the television in the dining room and catch up with the daily news. His ears pricked up at the appeal for any knowledge of an Englishman being seen in the area. The Police Nationale wanted to interview anyone fitting the description. An identikit picture flashed up on the screen. Claude's ears pricked up at the mention of an Englishman. They didn't get many in the town at this time of year. He peered at the identikit picture on the screen. He looked closer. The face did resemble the man who had booked in last evening. He wrote down the contact number and turned the television off as he heard his guests beginning to filter into the dining room for breakfast.

The last to sit down was Will Johnson. Claude took a good look at him as he showed him to his table.

"Bonjour, Mr. Johnson, please help yourself to breakfast," said Claude smiling pleasantly. "Do you wish tea or coffee?"

"Coffee please," answered Mick as he made his way to the buffet table.

When Claude saw that Mick was settled comfortably at his table with food and coffee he disappeared into his office at the back of the kitchen. He took a deep breath and then felt around in his pocket for the piece of paper with the number scribbled on it. He dialed the number and waited. Within seconds his call was answered. Speaking in French, Claude related how he believed the man they wanted to interview was staying at his establishment. He was instructed that the man could be dangerous and he was not to give any indication to the Englishman that he had notified the police. They would send two plain clothes policemen over to the hotel at once.

Claude walked back into the dining room to check on his guests as he did every morning. Mick was still drinking his coffee.

"Do you have an English newspaper?" Mick asked him.

"I'm sorry, Will," answered Claude, shaking his head. "I have to order the night before," he explained.

"Not to worry, can you just turn on the television. It's very quiet in here." Reluctantly Claude switched on the television.

"Can I have another coffee, Claude," requested Mick as he moved to a seat nearer the television. Claude was getting very nervous as he hurried into the kitchen to fetch the coffee.

"I wish the police would hurry up," he muttered to himself. The guests had finished their breakfasts and the dining room was empty, all except Mick who seemed in no hurry to make a move.

Suddenly Mick sat bolt upright in his chair.

"No," he muttered to himself. "This can't be happening. That bastard Tom has spilled his guts. I need to get out of here quick." What had alerted him was an identity picture not unlike himself on the television news and what he understood to be an appeal for information. He made his way straight to the kitchen; Claude was washing the breakfast dishes. He was unaware of anyone in the kitchen until Mick grabbed him.

"That's why you went all nervy when I asked you to turn on the television," he shouted at Claude. "You know, don't you? You have seen that picture and put two and two together. You think that's me, don't you?"

"I don't know what you mean, Monsieur. What are you talking about?" whimpered Claude, shaking with fright.

"If you've contacted the police, you're a dead man." Mick pulled out a gun and pointed it at Claude. Claude backed away, terrified.

"I need to get out of here," shouted Mick, keeping the gun trained on Claude. "Show me the back way out." At this point two plain clothes men entered the kitchen. Mick instinctively realised they were police officers.

"Back off, or I'll shoot him I swear." Mick was desperate. The police stood quite still and one of them tried to reason with Mick. He spoke good English.

"We only want to ask you a few questions," he told him calmly. "Put the gun down on the table. Don't make this any worse for yourself."

Mick was in a state of panic and kept the gun pointed at Claude. He had pictured himself in the South of France leading a new life and now this. He couldn't think straight beyond the fact that he held the ace card at the moment. The police had to go along with what he wanted as long as he held a gun. He dragged Claude in front of him and put the gun to his head. The police stood very still. After a few seconds the policeman who had spoken originally addressed Mick.

"Just put the gun down sir, and we will listen to what you have to say." Mick hesitated and still held the gun up against Claude's head. He was in a tight spot. He realised that French police carried guns. The situation was beginning to get out of hand. He didn't know what to do but he knew he had to keep his nerve. Claude was visibly shaking and was as white as a ghost. He shouted to the police to drop their guns on to the floor. Carefully they complied.

Mick was thinking fast as to what his next move would be. Even if he managed to get out of the immediate situation, he would be a marked man. He was stuck. A car. Yes, that's what he needed. As long as he had Claude with him as a hostage, he would have a safety net. He could swap the car when he had lost the police tailing him. He would then dump Claude, kill him if he had to. Yes, he had a plan.

"Right," Mick spoke at last. "Me and me lad'o here want a car with a full tank of petrol. If you put a tracker on it or I see any sign of you following me then he's a gonner."

"Think about this, sir," said the police officer calmly. "We only came in to ask you a few questions and to check on some information we have received. I ask you again to put the gun down. We can sort this out calmly."

"I don't believe you," shouted Mick. He was too stressed to reason with them. His only thought was of a car and freedom. "Just get me the car. My patience won't hold out much longer. I'll shoot the lot of you," he threatened, desperate and in a blind panic. The officers held up their hands.

"All right," said the spokesman." Have it your way. I'll have to use the phone though." Claude stared at the back room. Mick pointed the gun at all three of them.

"Two of you against the wall, and you," he pointed to the officer who had been doing all the talking. "You make the call and arrange a car. I want it now and no funny business," he warned. The officer dialled the number and began to speak in French.

"Speak in English," yelled Mick. The officer nodded and the arrangements were made to send a car straight to the hotel.

"Move to the front of the building, all of you," shouted Mick. "Don't forget, "I'm taking him with me and if you want him kept alive, you'll not follow us. You drive the car," he snarled at Claude. Within fifteen minutes a car arrived and a man got out.

"Careful, don't make any sudden moves," instructed Mick. He pointed the gun at Claude's head. "Just get in and start the engine. I'm right behind you." Claude carefully did as he was told and started up the engine. Just as Mick bent his head to get into the car a shot rang out from the building opposite. Mick fell to the floor. He dropped the gun and lay on the pavement, blood oozing from a wound in his chest. One of the officers quickly retrieved the gun. Claude scrambled out of the car and ran back over to the hotel. An ambulance siren sounded louder and louder as police held back the crowd of people who had gathered on the pavement. Soon the ambulance crew were bending over Mick.

"How come someone shot me?" Mick whispered breathlessly to the police officer who had accompanied him in the ambulance.

"You did it to yourself, "explained the officer. "You insisted I spoke to my colleagues in English. They knew we had gone to interview an Englishman and deduced it was you. They put a sniper in place in the building opposite the hotel. As soon as Claude was in the car, he could risk a shot." Mick's breathing was becoming laboured and the medic put an oxygen mask over his face to help him to breathe. Mick lay calmly and then took the mask off. Struggling for breath he pushed the medic away.

"I've had it," he whispered. Struggling to breathe he tried to sit up and speak. "I don't want to live." he gasped. "I was not fated to have a better life." He gasped again and struggled for breath. The medic held his hand. Mick was muttering to himself then fell unconscious. The medic put the mask on Mick's face again but his breathing became even more laboured and shallow. By the time they had reached the hospital, Mick was dead.

The police took Mick's passport and had duly notified Jenny of Mick's passing and of the circumstances of his death and she had been advised to get in touch with the British consul to make the necessary arrangements to have him brought home. She was shocked and bewildered as to why Mick had been living in a boarding house in France. Cathie recalled going to the funeral. She remembered standing by the graveside with Jenny and the girls. It was a cold wet miserable day. Cathie was only there to support Jenny. She would rather have stayed at home as by now everyone knew that her husband was behind bars.

"Ashes to ashes," the vicar droned on and Jenny dutifully threw a handful of soil on to the coffin. She had shown no emotion. She just stood at the graveside with her arms around her girls staring at the black hole that held the coffin.

"Come on," said Cathie. "It's no-good standing here Jen. Let's get you all back into the warmth. The girls are getting frozen." Dilys was sobbing and holding Anne's hand. Cathie led them away. Her friends and neighbours had come to the funeral to support Jenny. No-one had much respect for Mick except his parents. His mother was sobbing loudly. All the village knew the way he had cheated on his wife. They would have been more horrified if they had known of the beatings she had endured over the years.

A lonely figure stood at the back of the churchyard waiting for Jenny and her family to depart. Tears were rolling down her face. All their plans had come to nothing. She felt as though her whole world had fallen in on her. She would make her way over to the graveside to say her last goodbyes to her lover when everyone else had gone. What she didn't understand was, what was Mick doing in France?

Cathie and Jenny took the children back to Cathie's house. She had not wanted her own children to attend the funeral and she needed to be home before they came in from school. They didn't arrange a wake. There was little to celebrate in Mick's life, Jenny had reasoned. His parents, Mick's brothers and sisters, and a few families went for a drink in the local pub. Cathie and Jenny didn't want people probing and asking questions, trying to find out why Mick was dead, why was he in France and why wasn't Tom at the funeral?

When the children arrived home from school, Cathie asked Sarah to take some squash and biscuits into the front room and put on the television for Paul. Soon all the children were settled. Sarah did not question her mother, no doubt the children were asking each other about what had happened to their fathers and comforting each other. One father dead, one father missing.

Chapter Twenty-Three

Cathie and Jenny sat down in the kitchen over a cup of tea.

"I'm not sorry he's dead Cathie," Jenny stated. "I don't think the girls will pine for him very much. They hardly ever saw him. They are much closer to Gwilym these days."

"Thank goodness you have him in your life to turn too," remarked Cathie.

"I would manage even if I didn't." replied Jenny sharply. "I've had to bring the girls up and run the smallholding on my own for years. The only thing I'll miss is the money Mick gave us which wasn't much. Most of his wages went on that tart, Norma. But I have built up quite a little business on the market stall. I will have a widow's pension I suppose. I won't depend on Gwilym. I'll never make the mistake of depending on a man again. I can look after myself and the girls." She sounded very bitter. She took a breath and looked at her sister. "Perhaps Gwilym and I will get together properly one day but right now I want to feel the freedom of just having me and the girls to think about. I won't have to dread the sound of his truck coming down the lane and wondering what sort of mood I'll be facing. I'm glad he's dead. Am I being a hard bitch Cathie?" she asked. "After all I suppose I wouldn't have my two lovely girls if it wasn't for him."

"You're not hard Jen, You're strong. He made you that way. But don't dismiss Gwilym. He's a nice guy and is kind to you and the girls."

"Yes, I suppose he is," agreed Jenny. "I'm just a bit bitter.

And speaking of nice kind guys, your Tom was a fine example of a nice kind family man and look where he's ended up." Cathie stared at her sister and nodded.

"You're right Jen, not many men can be trusted. Tom cheated on me, Mick knew and blackmailed him. That's why he's in nick now." Jenny looked puzzled.

"I didn't realise," she said. Cathie continued.

"Tom wasn't going to take the wrap and groused to the police that Mick had planned a burglary that went wrong and he then kidnapped that girl. Tom was only supposed to be a getaway car."

Cathie spilt to Jenny all that Tom had told her about his affair, the consequent blackmailing and the kidnapping.

"Mick seemed hell-bent on getting a stash of money together Jenny. Tom told me Mick was intent on leaving you and the girls and was planning to take that Norma to Australia to start a new life. I'll never forgive Tom for all this. I've finished with him for good."

Jenny was taken aback. This was the first time she had heard of Mick's plans.

"Rotten bastard of a husband. I knew he was having an affair. I was glad. Kept him away from me and out of the house. But I didn't know he intended to move to the other side of the world. Well, that shows how much he thought of his daughters. I hope they don't mourn him for too long. I certainly won't. Did you see that Norma in the churchyard, Cathie? She was standing at the back waiting for us to go. She's had a happy release if only she knew it. One day I might tell her what he was really like to live with."

Tom had been on remand for twelve months before his trial came up at Chester Crown Court. Cathie had not visited him during that time. She was too angry. It had been so hard for her to break the news to the children that their father wouldn't be coming home any time soon.

Daniel, her solicitor, had informed her that Tom was going to plead guilty to all charges in the hope that this would go in his favour. The following evening when Paul was in bed, she broke the news gently to her two eldest children. She told them their father had been blackmailed into providing a car for their uncle Mick, who had taken Marianne hostage to get money from her father. As Tom had been a party to this crime he would be found just as guilty. The children were stunned to hear that their father was in prison. Luckily, they were too shocked to ask their mother what Tom was being blackmailed for so she didn't have to disillusion them further. Sarah cried herself to sleep that night, Cathie recalled angrily. Neil became very quiet and introvert following being told. He stayed away from all his out of school activities. He lost most of his friends. They all knew what his father had done. He was very unhappy and Cathie didn't know how to put it right. They would have to move.

She had not told Paul everything. All he knew was that his father was working away and would be gone for a long while. He accepted this explanation and his little life carried on as normal.

Cathie and Jenny attended the trial. Cathie felt physically sick as she stared at Tom as he was brought up from the cells and put in the dock accompanied by a prison officer. He had lost weight and looked ill. Jenny squeezed her hand tightly.

The barrister for the prosecution gave damning evidence

against Tom, explaining to the jury how the police had caught up with his car leaving the caravan site where the hostage was held. The hostage money and the victim's fingerprints were found in his car. The prisoner had admitted to everything and the barrister read out Tom's statement. It was a foregone conclusion that Tom would receive a long prison sentence.

In his defence, the lawyer defending Tom pointed out there were mitigating circumstances. His client was the victim of blackmail and had given evidence against Mick. He had told the police everything that had happened involving the kidnapping. He read out the statement.

The judge looked very surly. He did not look convinced by the plea from the defence lawyer. He addressed Tom.

"The lives of your wife and family were not at risk when you succumbed to blackmail, only your own comfortable lifestyle." he pointed out. "There was a choice. You chose the wrong path and put an innocent girl's life in grave danger. The law is the law and, on your admittance, you were an accomplice to armed robbery." He turned his attention to the jury and addressed them. "Armed robbery and the taking of a hostage are very serious crimes. Please retire to consider your verdict."

The jury returned after about two hours. The foreman told the judge that they had a unanimous verdict in finding the prisoner guilty as charged. Tom went deathly pale and glanced over to Cathie. She felt his eyes on her but kept looking straight ahead as he was taken back down to the cells.

The following week Tom was brought back into court for sentencing. He looked around for Cathie but she was not there. The judge gave him a sentence of seven years for assisting in an armed robbery and seven years for his part in the kidnapping of a young girl. The sentences were to run concurrently. He was told by his barrister that he may be released after he had served two-thirds of his sentence if he had a record of good behaviour.

Tom returned to his cell and lay on his bunk, too shocked to move.

It had been twelve months since Tom had been sentenced. He had been moved up to a men's prison in Durham so even if Cathie had the inclination to visit Tom, it would be a long drive. She had visited him twice only prior to the move. He was so contrite and remorseful over everything he had done, but Cathie felt no sympathy towards him. He had ruined their family and their business. They had lost everything they had worked for. The last visit had made her so angry. She resolved to take that anger to regain strength and determination to look after her children. She had been unaware at the beginning as to how desperate her situation was.

In the beginning she had tried to carry on the garage business with the help of Phil. She would carry on doing the book-keeping and drive the minibus when she could, but her heart was broken. She became extremely depressed. She struggled to get out of bed in the mornings to face the day and get the children ready for school. She picked at her food and she started to lose weight. She became a shadow of her former, cheerful self.

Phil was worried about her. He realized the business was losing money. Their local clients had read what Tom had been up to. The trial had been splashed across all the local papers. Many of them shunned the garage and took their business elsewhere. Finally, the day came when Phil and Cathie were forced to put the garage up for sale. The house held the collateral for a second mortgage on the garage and Cathie had to face the fact that not only was she to lose her livelihood but she would lose the house as well. She was now facing bankruptcy.

"All this time that waster of a husband of mine is tucked up in his warm little cell with television, snooker, three meals a day and no worries as to where the next penny is coming from. The only thing is he's not got is a key. He's doing, ok, isn't he?" Cathie was sounding off to her sister.

"Come on Cathie," replied Jenny. "He must be going through hell in there knowing all this is going on."

"Well, I haven't told him. I've no intention of telling him anything. He's no part of my life now. I've only gone to see him for the children's sake. They keep asking me if he's all right." Cathie was sobbing. Jenny looked at her, noticed the weight she had lost and how unkempt she had become. She had to take the reins here and help her sister and the children.

"Cathie, you have the date that the house has to go. Have you been looking at anywhere to rent yet?" Cathie stared at Jenny.

"I can't face it Jenny. It's like a nightmare and I keep hoping I'll wake up." Jenny took hold of her sister's hand.

"Cathie love, this is real. It's not going to go away. I've been thinking. Why don't you and the kids come and stay with me for a little while? I can put a bit of your furniture in the barn and it's not too far to drive the kids to school. What do you think? We can apply to the council for housing in the meantime?" She waited for Cathie's reaction. A look of relief spread over Cathie's face.

"Oh Jenny, could you do that. I don't know which way to turn at the moment. My head is going round in circles. I sometimes think I am losing my mind."

So, it was settled. Jenny and Cathie and all the children stayed together on the smallholding. Jenny loved having the house full. Cathie started to regain some weight. Her children were happier and seemed to forget for a while that their Dad was not with them as they helped their cousins to look after the chickens and calves.

After about six months Cathie received a letter from the local council. As the number of people in Jenny's house was classed as overcrowding, they were offering Cathie a three bedroomed house on an estate not too far from their schools.

"Some good news at last," said Cathie excitedly. "It seems ideal. Shall we go over and take a look at the weekend?" On the Sunday they drove over to the estate. It looked peaceful enough although there were a few scrapped cars in some driveways and a few dogs roaming around. They had been given a set of keys and they eagerly opened the front door. Cathie noticed curtains moving over the road but it didn't bother her.

The children ran around the house opening doors and exploring.

"Bags this bedroom, shouted Neil. It's the biggest but I'll have to share with Paul I expect." Cathie nodded.

"It does seem ok, Jenny. There's carpets and curtains here already and they don't look at all bad."

"That's a good thing," replied Jenny. "They don't give you much to live on at the social. You can probably get your rent paid if you apply." Cathie shuddered. She had never had to depend on handouts before.

"We'll manage till I can get a job," she answered. "It's a new start." She hugged Jenny.

"We'll miss having you and the girls around but we have to stand on our own feet sometime. I'm quite excited. Perhaps Gwilym will help me bring my furniture over."

Within two weeks Cathie and the children had settled into their new home. Cathie was feeling more secure but within a month problem started to arise. Neil started staying out late, was evasive when Cathie questioned where he had been and with whom. He became secretive and had a bad attitude towards her. She suspected he had started smoking and challenged him.

"What if I have," Neil snapped back defiantly. "Everyone here smokes. I didn't ask to live here and I don't want to be the odd one out."

"Where are you getting them from?" persisted his mother. "Cigarettes cost more than the pocket money I give you."

"Oh, I do odd jobs here and there," was the vague answer.

Neil's behaviour was becoming more erratic. Cathie suspected it was more than cigarettes he was smoking. She suspected it was cannabis. One afternoon a few weeks later she had seen Neil laughing and joking with a gang of boys she knew to be troublemakers. She had tried to call him away on the pretext of going to the shop for her. The boys just laughed and Neil turned his back on her. She knew then that coming to this estate was a mistake. Her children had led sheltered lives and would be easily led by local gangs.

Cathie felt trapped. She had been on this rough estate for

about twelve months. She still had Paul at home so full-time work would be difficult until he reached five in a few months' time. She would have to take a refresher course to take up her nursing skills again. Meanwhile she had sleepless nights worrying over what her eldest son was up to. She put on a brave face whenever Jenny phoned. She felt her sister had done enough. She had to learn to stand on her own two feet.

The evening Neil got into the fight and she was hit across her face by some boy's mother was the night everything changed. Cathie had tried to make the best of things and put on a brave face in front of the children but her mental health was suffering once more. That evening she sat crying and drinking and reflecting over her failed marriage and the lifestyle she and the children were now forced to live. The woman assaulting her was the last straw. She opened another bottle of wine and tried to blot out the past.

The next day she managed to get the two children to school, came home and just sat and stared out of the window. She had no energy or interest in cleaning the house or attending to Paul. She sat him in front of the television and went back to staring out of the window, tears rolling down her face. When Neil and Sarah came home Sarah tried to coax her mother into getting a meal ready whilst Sarah cleaned up the house. Neil took no interest in helping or talking to his mother. He disappeared out for the evening.

"Save me some tea," he called out to Sarah as he went out of the door. Sarah sorted out some clothes for the next day, then busied herself getting tea ready, whilst Cathie sat and stared out of the window.

"Come on, Mum," Sarah tried to chivvy her up. "This is not

like you. Paul and me are hungry. Help me with tea." Cathie seemed to respond and slowly went into the kitchen to help Sarah.

As the days went by, Cathie sank lower and lower into a depressive state. One late afternoon there was a knock on the door. Sarah went to answer it. Cathie would neither answer the door or go outside since she had been assaulted. Sarah answered the door to two women.

"Can we come in," they enquired.

"I don't think mum wants to see anyone," Sarah told them but they were already over the doorstep. They identified themselves and confirmed they were talking to Sarah's mother.

"We are from Social Services," they told her. "I am Miss Williams and this is my assistant Mrs. Harris. We've had complaints from the school your children attend. Your children are getting to school late; they are untidy and hungry every morning and their homework is not getting done. The headmaster is a bit worried that things are difficult at home."

Cathie just sat cuddling Paul and then she began to cry, rocking to and fro. Sarah ran over and put her arms around her mother.

"We are worried about you and your family, Mrs. Blackwood. You are not well and we don't think you or the children are eating properly. You will all be ill before long," stated Miss Williams. Sarah spoke up.

"I am looking after our mam. She has had a lot of worries. I can look after my brothers 'till she's better."

"But mum looks very ill Sarah," persisted Miss Williams.

"We think she may have to go into hospital for a while." Cathie just stared around her, rocking to and fro.

"We are going to arrange for your mother to go into hospital for a little while," Miss Williams told Sarah quietly. "We will find a nice foster home for you and your brothers in the meantime. You cannot stay here on your own. We will make sure you all stay together and you won't have to move schools." Sarah thought quickly.

"Our Auntie will let us stay there. I know she will. We stayed there when we lost our home. We don't want to go anywhere strange. Please ask her." Sarah was desperate.

"Well, that would be an answer," agreed Miss Williams. I will ring her if you find the number."

Jenny was shocked to hear how her sister had slid into a state of severe depression once more.

"I'll come over at once," she said, "The children can come home with me for as long as it takes for my sister to recover. And so, it was arranged and after one or two phone calls an ambulance arrived to take Cathie to the psychiatric hospital. The children gave their mother hugs and then Jenny led them back into the house to pack their clothes and return once more to their cousins on the smallholding.

Chapter Twenty-Four

Under the care of a psychiatrist and with counselling and regular meals, Cathie's mental health started to improve. Her children seemed happy and visited regularly. Neil had lost his hostile attitude and chatted about his work helping out on the smallholding. Cathie began to look forward to the children's visits and started to think about her future. Jenny seemed happy to have the children and not to have the worry of Mick in her life.

Everything seemed to be on a positive note and one day Cathie told her councilor that she thought she was ready to go out and face the world again. The councillor agreed but advised Cathie not to go back to her house but to stay with her sister for a while. Cathie took all the advice given and moved in once more with her sister.

When she had been there for a week, Jenny told her she needed to tell her something. Cathie felt a knot in her stomach. She sat down.

"I don't think I can deal with bad news yet, Jenny. It's not Tom, is it?" she asked anxiously.

"No love, no-one has died. It's something that we can fix but you have to know."

"Go on then," replied Cathie taking a deep breath.

"I have been keeping an eye on your house," said Jenny. "Last week when I went over the front door was open. I phoned the police. When they checked the whole house had been ransacked. The television and radio were gone and all your jewellery." Cathie gasped. "Luckily your photos and clothes were still there but scattered everywhere. They had taken everything of any value." Cathie laughed bitterly.

"Well, that wouldn't be much. We lost most things when we gave up the house. I'm not upset Jenny. As long as no one has been hurt. We can replace our things. I wouldn't have liked them to have touched my photos though. This is a minor setback to what we have been through. I expect it's kids looking for drug money."

Jenny was relieved that she had told her and that it hadn't seem to have set her back.

"I can't face going back there anyway, Jenny," Cathie admitted to her sister. "I don't know what to do. I can't impose on you indefinitely."

"You stay as long as you like," said Jenny. I love having you all here."

"What about Gwilym?" asked Cathie. "He must be fed up with all of us taking up your time."

"Well, he'll have to put up with it," replied Jenny. "Family comes first. We'll phone the council in the morning and tell them they can give the house to someone else."

Cathie gathered her children around her that evening.

"You'll be glad to hear we can stay with your Auntie Jenny for the time being. She turned to her eldest. "Sarah has been the backbone of this family since your Dad went away. Now I want you to step up and be the man of the family. There are lots of jobs that you can be doing around here."

"I'm sorry mam if I made you ill. I will work harder at school and around here and try to make you proud of me." Cathie smiled at her son.

"You didn't make me ill. It was lots of things. You are a good boy and I have every faith in you. And as for you young man," she said turning to Paul. "You are coming up five. Quite grown up. You will be going to school next term and I will be going back to work. Now let's pop down to the chip shop and we can all have a special tea to celebrate."

The next morning Cathie got up early, took the children to school and bought the local paper. She scanned the job vacancy page over a cup of coffee. There was nothing suitable. She didn't have the confidence to apply to the local hospital after everything that had happened. She felt very ashamed and had the notion that everyone would be talking about her. 'One day' she resolved.

One day I will be able to put this all behind me and hold my head up high again. But not yet. Over the next few weeks, she scanned the papers for a job she felt confident enough to undertake.

At last, she found an advert which she thought she could apply for. The advert was asking for a carer to look after a gentleman in his own home.

I won't have to face people and answer difficult questions' Before she lost her nerve, she picked up the phone and rang the number. The man sounded pleasant enough on the phone and he arranged an interview for two o clock the next day.

The next day she headed off to the address he had given her. It was a large house standing in its own grounds. She knocked at the door and was shown into the hall by an elderly lady.

"I'm Mrs. Evans, Mr. Edwards' housekeeper," the lady

introduced herself. Cathie introduced herself and was shown into a large room at the front of the house where sitting in an armchair was a frail man of about seventy. He was quite thin but sat quite upright. He had a trimmed moustache and Cathie thought he had the look of an ex-military man. He called her over and indicated that she sit down on the settee opposite.

"You're Cathie I presume?" he enquired.

"Yes, I am," she answered. "And you must be Mr. Edwards?"

"That's right," he smiled at her. "But please call me Richard." Over tea and biscuits, they got to know a bit about each other. Richard had indeed been in the Armed Services. He had served twenty-two years as an officer in the guards and had a rank of captain which he refrained from using. On examining Cathie's references, he was pleased to learn that she was also ex-Army. They spent a while reminiscing over their military days before getting back to the subject in hand. Richard told her he had been diagnosed with bowel cancer eighteen months ago. He had undergone one operation to remove the tumour but unfortunately the cancer had spread. He seemed quite calm and resigned to the fact that he was terminally ill.

"I see you drive," he said. "That is quite important. Since my wife died a year ago, I have not felt up to going out, but if I had company it would make a difference. I do have a lady who comes in four days a week for a few hours to clean and do a meal for me and any shopping I need. I require a companion more than a nurse at this stage but there will come a time when I will need more nursing care and I would like it to be with someone I knew. I don't plan to end my days in a hospital surrounded by strangers." Cathie's heart went out to this frail lonely old man.

"I would like to take the job, Richard, if you think I am suitable. Shall I ring you when you have had time to think about it?" asked Cathie. Richard looked at her.

"I don't need to think about its Cathie. I liked you on sight and I think I can trust you. Tell me more about your home circumstances and then we can discuss hours and wages."

Cathie left the house feeling very pleased with herself. She would work for Richard around school hours to start with and then increase her hours as necessary. Neil was coming up to fifteen now and Sarah thirteen. They were well able to collect Paul from school and make themselves a snack if she worked longer.

When she arrived back at the smallholding, she couldn't wait to tell Jenny all about it. She was so excited.

"Get the kettle on Jenny. It's good news at last." She told her sister all about Richard and his circumstances and how they had arranged that she could fit her working hours around her own commitments.

"Wonderful," agreed Jenny. "It's time you had some good luck."

"I've been thinking while I've been driving over," Cathie carried on. "When I've earned my first month's pay, I'm going to look for a flat for me and the kids and try to get some normality back into our lives."

"But we love having you here Cath. You don't have to think about getting a place to live," Jenny sounded disappointed.

"I hope you can understand that I want to stand on my own feet, Jenny. I'll be eternally grateful to you for all you have done for us but I feel much stronger now. I believe I can even face driving up to visit Tom in a few weeks. I kind of feel sorry for him now after mulling it all over. I know he had an affair, but it didn't last long and look at the price he has had to pay. Mick blackmailed him and Tom put the money they stole back into the business to keep us from going under."

"You don't have to justify going to see him love," Jenny told her. "Mick was a bad bastard and just roped Tom in. I know that. It doesn't do to hold grudges forever. It just makes you bitter. Mick paid the ultimate price for his greed. Mind you, I have no sympathy for him. He can't hurt me anymore. Tom is of a different mould. You go and see him Cathie when you are ready."

"Thanks for not thinking me stupid, Jenny. The kids do miss him and they would appreciate me going to see him. I do encourage them to write to him and he must look forward to his mail. He always writes straight back. The kids idolize their father and he has always been a good Dad."

Cathie was enjoying her new job. It was more like visiting a friend and getting paid for it. She got on well with Richard. They went on local trips together when he was feeling well and when it was raining, she read to him and he taught her to play chess. When they were out, they laughed and chatted together. Richard liked to sit in the park and watch the children playing.

"My wife and I used to watch people and try to guess what was happening in their lives. We never knew the answers of course, Cathie," he laughed. "We did fantasize a lot and made up some exciting stories."

"Sounds fun," Cathie agreed and thought to herself that she could come out with a few stories that would surprise him but she had to keep all that to herself.

One afternoon Richard made the suggestion that Cathie may like to bring the children over one Saturday to meet him. She had told him all about them.

"I would like to," replied Cathie. "I do tell them about our trips out and that you were in the Army." She made a mental note to remind the children that their father had left them when they were little. That was the story she had told Richard and she didn't want any awkward questions being asked.

After a couple of months had passed, Cathie had found a suitable three bedroomed flat for them not far from the schools. It was partly furnished and she and Jenny took the rest of Cathie's furniture over from the smallholding. They went shopping for new curtains and bedding and soon the flat was looking very cosy.

"My own front door at last," sighed Cathie.

"And in a nice neighbourhood," added Jenny. "No gangs prowling around the streets."

"It's lovely Mum," said Sarah and Neil nodded in agreement.

The following weekend Richard felt well enough to ask the children to visit on the Saturday afternoon. He had asked Mrs. Jones to get in some ice cream, crisps, cakes and lemonade and lay it out before they came so he could give them a little buffet tea. The children had been warned to be on their best behaviour and they were very polite when they met him. Cathie was impressed. She had worried that Paul would start misbehaving if he got bored but all went well. After the first visit the children went over to visit Richard every other week when he was well. He and the children looked forward to the visits. He taught them to play draughts and different card games with the eldest and bought a supply of Dinky cars to keep Paul amused.

Cathie had requested a visiting order to see Tom. It was a long drive up to Durham. She had lots to think about on the way. The children were left behind with Jenny for two days as she had booked in to a hotel for the night.

She was on edge as she entered the prison. She had not seen Tom since he had been moved and she recalled that she had told him that she never wanted to see him again.

"Hello, Cathie," he began as they sat down opposite one another. He couldn't meet her eyes, but kept looking down. "It's so good to see you. I honestly believed you never wanted to see me again. What changed your mind?"

"Look at me Tom, and stop staring at the floor," said Cathie. She looked him in the eyes. "Oh, I did mean it, believe me," she told him. "You have destroyed everything and I can't trust you ever again. It has been so hard for the kids. Paul still cries at night and wonders where you are. He wet the bed for a while but is settling better now. Our Jenny pulled us through and we are coping now at last." She didn't feel she could elaborate on what had gone on. Tom looked down at the table again.

"I don't know what to say to you Cathie. I can never make it right. I will never forgive myself for what I have done to my family. I lie awake at night thinking about what a complete ass I have been. I deserve everything I've got." Cathie nodded.

"Yes, you do Tom." She then told him where the council had put them when she lost the house and how Neil had got into trouble and if it hadn't been for Jenny the kids would have been put into care and would probably be still there. She was angry now and decided to tell him everything. She didn't hold back. He needed to hear it all. Tom just kept staring at the table. He remained silent.

Finally, she told him about her job and the new flat and that they were settled at last. Neil had a new set of friends now and played football most Sundays.

"This proves I can run my life without you, Tom," she told him bitterly. "I don't need you. But I have decided that I will not interfere with your relationship with the children."

"I look forward to their letters and thank you for the photos of them you sent. It keeps me going in here looking forward to the post."

"Well, I won't stop that," replied Cathie. The visit came to an end and they awkwardly said goodbye to one another. Tom staring at the door as she left without a backward glance.

Cathie was shaking as she left the prison. Mixed emotions were running around in her head. Surprisingly her heart had skipped a beat when she first saw Tom and she felt sympathy towards him as she realized how contrite he was.

Get a grip. Remember what he has done. Never rely on anyone again and you won't get hurt. 'She clenched her fists angrily.

She was calmer and more determined than ever not to feel sorry for Tom as she sat down with a glass of wine later that evening. She had made no plans to see him again for a while. She had to get on with her own life now.

As the weeks went by, Richard's health started to deteriorate.

He felt too tired to manage trips out in the car any longer. The children still visited him on Saturdays if he was well enough as he so looked forward to seeing them.

"He needs me a lot more now Jenny," Cathie confided to her sister. "I think he needs attention during the night as well. He shouldn't be on his own. He's needing more morphine and I'm afraid he may fall."

"You'll have to discuss your concerns with him, Cathie. See what he feels. He's a very proud man and will struggle on without saying anything if you let him."

The next afternoon Cathie made them both a cup of tea and gently informed Richard that they must take the next step in his future care.

"I know I haven't got much longer," Richard admitted. Cathie's eyes filled with tears. She had grown very fond of him.

"I've been thinking, Cathie. What if you and the children move in here with me. There's plenty of room. I would pay the rent on your flat for a while. You don't have to give it up. You have become like family to me. I was pretty lonely after my wife died. We were never blessed with children as you know. You and the children have made me very happy these last few months. I don't want to die in hospital." Cathie leant over and took hold of his hands. They were cold. He looked very frail, and his eyes were desperately pleading for her answer. She did not hesitate.

"We would like nothing better than to be here with you Richard. The children think the world of you. Are you sure they won't be too much for you?"

"I would love to have the children around me," Richard

sounded relieved. "They will take my mind off thinking about myself."

Cathie explained to the children that they were going to move in with Richard as he needed more care now. She told the two eldest that Richard was very poorly and he would not get better. Sarah cried when she heard but Neil said he had guessed that anyway and life could be pretty cruel, losing his Dad and now his friend. Cathie hugged them both, glad that she had forewarned them. She had not told little Paul. She would have to face that one when the time came.

Cathie organized the move and gave the children their instructions.

"You can have your bedrooms as we had them in the flat. I will have the bedroom next to Richard so I can hear him if he is awake in the night. You have to respect Richard's house and not be too noisy."

"Why do we have to move in here?" enquired Paul. Sarah answered.

"Because Mummy's a nurse and she wants to look after Richard properly as he is now so poorly. He doesn't want to leave us and have to go into hospital. Everything will be the same. You can have your games and Dinky cars. You will just sleep here instead of in our flat." Paul seemed to accept the explanation. "Richard has bought you a garage with a lift for your cars. He'll show you how it works at the weekend. You can put it together with him."

"Wow," said Paul impressed. He clapped his hands together.

"He spoils you," smiled Cathie. "Now go and wash your hands before tea."

That weekend they all moved into Richard's house. Cathie and Sarah shared a room and Neil and Paul shared. Cathie took the room next to Richard's so she could hear him if he needed her in the night. She had given him a bell to ring and she hoped he would use it. He did tend to doze off more in the daytime now. He was taking morphine to keep him as free from pain as possible. Cathie helped him with washing and dressing and cooked him the meals he fancied. He was getting visibly weaker as the weeks went by.

The children seemed to recognize how ill he was and they went about the house quietly if they saw he was sleeping. They popped in to see him when he was awake. Richard seemed calm and content to have Cathie and the children in the house. Cathie read to him sometimes and the doctor popped in regularly to check if he was having any pain.

Cathie began checking on him a couple of times during the night. She needed to know he was still breathing. He seemed to sleep most of the time now. He was very weak and eating very little. One night she had a feeling his time was immanent and as soon as he had drifted off to sleep, she settled herself in a chair by his bedside in case he needed her. This became her regular routine over the next few days. One night his breathing became very erratic and noisy and then became very shallow. She reached over and called his name but he did not respond. Richard had slipped into a coma from which he did not recover. The next night Richard passed away peacefully. As soon as she realized what had happened Cathie broke down and began to sob. After a few minutes she pulled herself together and telephoned the doctor. He arrived to confirm Richard's death and arranged undertakers to take Richard to the chapel of rest.

The children were wide awake with all the comings and

goings on. Cathie had to break the news to them that Richard had passed away. They were quite upset, especially Paul.

"Where is Richard, Mummy?" he asked. "Where has he gone? Daddy's gone, now Richard's gone. Have we done something bad Mummy? Where are they?" Sarah gave Paul a hug.

"We've not done anything wrong, Paul," she explained. "Daddy is away working, remember and Richard was very tired and has gone to live with Jesus in heaven. He can still see us from heaven but we won't be able to see him. When someone gets very sick and tired Jesus likes to take care of them himself." Paul thought about this and seemed satisfied with Sarah's explanation.

"You can all have the day off school today and go back to bed and try and get a bit more sleep. I'll phone the school." Cathie nodded to Sarah and Neil to take Paul back to bed.

Richard had nominated Cathie as his next of kin as he had no living relatives, so it fell on her shoulders to arrange the funeral and contact the solicitor to see if there were funds to cover the cost.

Cathie had made an appointment to see Mr. Thomas, Richard's solicitor. The elderly, stout gentleman sitting behind his desk got up and shook her hand warmly.

"I'm glad to meet you Mrs Blackwood," he said in a broad Welsh accent. "Mr Edwards was always singing your praises every time we met. You and your children made his last days very happy, you know."

"I'm glad to hear that," answered Cathie. "He was a real gentleman and we all grew to love him. We will miss him very much."

"Well, he was very poorly as you know. Now my secretary tells me you are worried about whether there are enough funds to cover the cost of the funeral. Let me reassure you dear. It's all provided for. And after the funeral, I would like you to make another appointment with me for the reading of the will. "Of course," answered Cathie not really taking in what he was saying. She was so relieved there was money to give Richard the send-off he deserved. To be buried alongside his beloved wife, Emily.

The day of the funeral was cold and damp. Dark clouds hung low. A day when it didn't seem to get any lighter. The coffin was carried in to the strains of a favourite piece of music that Cathie and Richard used to listen to sometimes in the afternoons. The service was attended by a few friends and neighbours. Cathie had left Paul with Jenny. The vicar talked about Richard and the days when Richard and Emily were regular churchgoers and involved in many church activities. They sang a hymn and then Richard was interred with his wife. As Cathie watched Richard being lowered into the ground her heartfelt like breaking. What would she do now without him?

Chapter Twenty-Five

Cathie and the children moved back into their own flat and Richard's house was locked up. Cathie scanned the papers each morning. She had to find a job quickly. The rent was due. One morning she suddenly remembered that the solicitor had asked her to make an appointment to see him after the funeral. She arranged to see him the following week.

"Come in Mrs Blackwood," greeted Mr Thomas. "Nice to see you again." Cathie sat down as Mr Thomas shuffled some papers around on his desk. "I have Richard's will here somewhere," he muttered to himself.

"Oh yes, here we are. As you know," he began. "Mr. Edwards had no known relatives and he appointed you next of kin."

"Yes," Cathie nodded. "Thank goodness I was able to carry out his wishes for his funeral."

"He thought a lot of you, Cathie. I think you became like a daughter to him. He came in here about six months ago and asked me to change his will. Originally he had left all his estate to the hospital."

"Yes, he told me that," agreed Cathie.

"Well, he obviously didn't tell you this, Mrs Blackwood. He changed his will so that all his money went to the hospital but he has left the house to you."

"What!" said Cathie. "I had no idea he had done that." She looked quite shocked.

"He wanted you and the children to have security after he had gone and this was the way he could ensure that. So now you own a three bedroomed property." Cathie's felt very emotional.

"Oh Richard. What a kind man. I hope I made him comfortable in his last year."

"You and the children made him extremely happy. He told me so. I'll arrange for the deeds of the house to be made over to you and you can move in whenever you like."

Cathie left the office, her head reeling. She made her way over to see Jenny.

"You'll never guess what has happened Jenny. Richard has gone and left me his house in his will. I'd no idea. He told me he was leaving everything to the hospital when he asked me to be his next of kin."

"Good heavens, Cathie," replied Jenny. "I knew he thought the world of you. What a lovely thing to have done. You did look after him like he was your own father. I think he thought of you as a daughter."

"That's what the solicitor said. Oh Jenny," she hugged her sister. "I've got security again for the kids. It's a big house. I can't believe it."

"Well," said Jenny. "You deserve it after all you've been through, losing the house and Tom in prison. You have choices now. To go back to nursing or down another path."

"Yes, I do. I can take my time now. I am just relieved I don't have to rush into taking any job just to pay the rent. I'll tell the kids tonight and see where we go from here."

Cathie looked at her sister.

"Now tell me your news. How are you managing? How are you getting on with Gwilym?" Jenny hesitated.

"We are jogging along. We still see one another but I find it very hard to commit to anything He wants us to marry but I am not sure and he gets annoyed. We have been rowing lately. I just like my freedom and my independence after years of abuse from Mick. Gwilym doesn't seem to understand. I find it hard to trust another man."

"I agree with you there," laughed Cathie. "We're not very good at choosing our men, are we?"

Now Richard was at peace Cathie's thoughts turned back to Tom. She felt guilty that she had not taken the children to see him but the thought of them seeing him supervised by prison wardens and them not being able to give their father a hug filled her with dread. But she knew she had to face it. It was not fair on the children. She discussed it with the two eldest and told them about the prison rules and they all decided it was no place for a seven-year-old and they would have to leave Paul with Jenny. Jenny would look after Paul for the two days they would be away. He didn't make a fuss or ask where they were going. He was eager to spend time on the smallholding. Jenny had obtained a rescue pony and had promised Paul that she would teach him to ride.

Tom sat waiting for his family to arrive. He had not seen his children since he had received his jail sentence three years and three long months ago. He didn't know what to say or how they would react to seeing him. His stomach was churning over. Then he caught sight of them as they entered the visiting room. Cathie held back and let the children speak to him first. Neil didn't know what to say to him and it was Sarah who broke the ice and smiled at her father. Cathie had prepared them with the fact that there must be no bodily contact. No hugs.

"I'm so glad to see you both. You can't imagine how I've missed you. And you have both grown up so much. I look forward to your letters each week but can't wait to get out of this place and see all of you together. How is Paul? I bet he has shot up too." He turned to Cathie as she sat down beside the children.

"We are all fine. I didn't think it right to bring Paul." Cathie explained.

"I understand," replied Tom. "And thank you for sending me the photos of him."

"He is learning to ride," Sarah piped up. "Auntie Jenny has a rescue pony. He is a Shetland called Robbie."

"He'll love that," laughed Tom. "Perhaps I can have a photo of him sat on Robbie." The atmosphere became more relaxed as the afternoon wore on. Cathie told Tom about Richard's will and the house and that she was now thinking of training to become a district nurse as she could now afford to go back to training.

Tom sat quietly thinking to himself how well his family was getting on without him. He tried to suppress the feeling of resentment that was overriding his enjoyment of the afternoon. He had to face the fact that although it was unsaid, they no longer needed him. He had to get on to a more positive note before the afternoon was ruined. He told them he was studying hard and had the opportunity to take a course with a diploma at the end of it on landscape gardening and horticulture. "I want to get away from mechanics and cars," he explained. "That line of work holds nothing but bad memories for me. I want a completely new start."

"I'm glad you are taking an interest in something. Your time in here will pass all the quicker. Will you be a fully-fledged landscape gardener when you leave here?"

"Oh yes," said Tom enthusiastically, relieved that Cathie had taken an interest. "Oh yes. It takes two years to finish the course and what I do have in here is time. And it gets me out in the open air to work in the gardens." The afternoon passed and the visit came to an end.

"We miss you Dad. Can't wait for you to come home," said Sarah, her eyes filling up with tears.

"I know, love," replied Tom. "I miss you all dreadfully too. But don't waste your tears on me. It's all my own fault but I will make it up to you all one day, I promise." he said looking at Cathie.

"Goodbye Tom," replied Cathie her eyes not meeting his. "We'll try not to make it so long between visits next time." And with that she and the children left the room. She was determined to show no emotion. Tom felt so deflated and sorry for himself as he went back to his cell, lay on his bunk staring at the bars on the window.

Sarah couldn't stop crying as they made their way back to the car. She had seen the look on her Dad's face as Cathie had left showing no feeling towards him.

"Dry your eyes Sarah," said Cathie sharply. "We'll arrange another visit in a little while."

"You hate him, don't you?" observed Neil.

"I don't hate him, Neil," Cathie sighed. "I don't hate your father. Hate is too strong a word. I am just so disappointed about what has happened to our family." Nobody spoke on the way back, each harbouring their own thoughts about how the day had gone and how they would cope as a family in the future.

Cathie and the children moved into the big house. It was strange and sad without Richard. She closed the door on his bedroom and couldn't go in there. She would have to in time, she told herself but not yet. Little by little she began to furnish the house with her own things. She found it very difficult. The neighbours were none too friendly when they found out that the house had been left to Cathie. She took no notice. She knew in her heart that she had made him happy and that was the reason he did it. The neighbours did little for him prior to her arrival and if they said anything to her, she wouldn't hesitate to tell them. She was a lot stronger now than when she had lived on the rough estate.

She thought more about taking up her career again and decided she would definitely like to train to qualify as a district nurse. It was a much-needed service and she could help people in the same situation as Richard. She could get a lot of job satisfaction from nursing patients in their own homes and she vowed not to make the mistake of getting too involved. She applied for the course and got her reply for an interview within a couple of weeks.

The interview was successful. The hours were a bit erratic but Neil and Sarah both volunteered to look after Paul when needed. She threw herself into studying for her new career. When she had a few days off Cathie took Neil and Sarah to visit their father again. The visit went better. Tom was enthusiastic about his courses and Cathie was telling Tom about her work on the district. There was no tension and Sarah didn't get too upset when the visit came to an end. Tom was a little more hopeful that given time Cathie may find it in her heart to forgive him. He loved and missed her so much.

Cathie concentrated on her work and studies and within two years she was a fully qualified district nurse. She now had a steady income and her own house. She could look forward to having a holiday break with the children and put money away for her children's future.

She threw all her energies into her job and looked forward each day to visiting her list of patients, listening to their problems and hoping that her visits cheered up the lonely ones. She never forgot those days when she couldn't find the will to get out of bed. If she saw depression or loneliness in any of her patients, she would go out of her way to put them in contact with advisors and volunteers who could make their lives happier.

Neil was studying hard at school. He had his heart set on joining the Army like his father and hoped to get good grades in his school exams. Sarah had her heart set on going to university to study law. She wanted to be a solicitor. Cathie had been putting money away to prepare for her children's further education. Paul was doing well at school and had begun to take a keen interest in Rugby.

"I want to play for Wales one day, Mam," he told her.

"That would be wonderful," she told him. She was so proud of all her children. They had been through so much and were so positive in their outlook on life.

Cathie had plans now to take the children to see their father every three months. It didn't upset her to see him anymore. She just had to suppress any emotional feelings she had towards him. The children felt at ease with the visits now and the last time they went they had prepared Paul and had taken him. He was so happy to see his father again. The children chatted away and told Tom all their news whilst Cathie sat and listened. She could feel Tom's eyes on her at times and knew he was longing for a smile from her or some softness between them but she didn't feel she should give him any false hopes.

Finally, when Tom had served nine years of his sentence the parole board granted his release under the supervision of a probation officer. As the date grew nearer Cathie felt that she wanted to visit Tom on her own to tell him what her intended plans were for their family. He was very apprehensive, hoping against hope that she would take him back. She faced Tom in that visiting room, with the table between them for the very last time at the prison. She had made up her mind what she was going to tell him and trusted that her heart would let her.

Chapter Twenty-Six

The years had passed and her eldest children were forging lives of their own. There was only Paul at home now. Neil had his wish and had been in the Army for a year. He had joined the Parachute Regiment like his father and was training hard for promotion. Sarah had worked hard for good grades in her exams and had been accepted to Cardiff university to study law.

"Tom," she began. She hesitated. "It doesn't feel right that you should come back to live with me as if nothing has happened. Our marriage has been badly damaged. I don't trust you and I can't share a bed with you feeling as I do." She waited for his reaction. Tom looked very disappointed but, in his heart, he knew what she would say.

"I understand completely Cath. I had a feeling this was coming. I realise how much I've hurt you. I've had years to think of what I did to you and the kids. And now you all manage perfectly well without me. I can't hope to come back into your lives as if nothing has happened. I 'm not stupid. But I now have qualifications for a different trade and my probation officer has been putting feelers about. I have not put a foot wrong since I have been in here and he thinks he has got me a job in a garden centre in Knutsford. It's a start. I would like to have my own business again one day, but I need a lot more experience in this line of work. I will get my own flat for the present and if it's all right with you I can visit the kids or have them over for a weekend here and there. I've talked this all over with the probation officer and if you agree he doesn't see why this won't work." He waited for her answer.

Cathie was relieved to hear his plans. She thought he would want to come home straight from the prison and slot back into family life. She wasn't ready for that at the moment. He had to prove to her and to himself that he could be a decent, responsible father to their children.

"I agree, Tom," she said. "This is going to take time so best we take things slowly." They ended the visit amicably and for the first time in many months Cathie turned around and smiled at him as she left.

Tom's probation officer found him a two bedroomed flat near to the garden centre where he would be working. He would be able to walk to his job.

He found life very strange when he was first released from prison. The thing he enjoyed most was being able to shut his own front door at night and be at peace. He kept himself to himself at work and his colleagues gave up asking him questions. All they knew was he had been working up north and had come to live in Cheshire to be nearer his relatives.

Cathie had brought the children to stay with him on his first weekend off. The sleeping arrangements were a bit squashed, with Tom ending up on the sofa, but he was so happy to have them with him. Nothing mattered now, only the freedom to work and to see his children. He and Cathie spoke amicably but there was no closeness coming from her. He tried not to let it upset him. He hoped that time would heal their broken marriage.

One morning when Tom had been in the job about six months he was called into the office. He was very apprehensive and relieved when the manager informed him that they were very pleased with his reliability and his approach to the job. Due to his qualifications he was to assist the head gardener who managed the landscaping side of the business.

"We are putting our trust in you," the manager informed him. "Don't let us down." Tom assured him he would not let anybody down in future.

'I have learned a hard lesson,' he thought to himself.

The landscaping work gave Tom the much-needed experience he required to even think about becoming self-employed again. It would be a while before he could approach a bank for the capital he needed. He would just have to be patient and carry on with what he was doing. If he was honest with himself, it was debatable if any bank would put their trust in him if they found out what he had done.

Fate intervened one morning later in the year. The children were visiting Tom and they had planned a trip to the coast. By this time, he had bought an old banger of a car and spent his evenings doing it up.

"Has Mum told you," enquired Sarah. Tom looked puzzled.

"Told me what?" He shook his head. "Mum doesn't talk to me much about anything except what she has too regarding you kids," he replied sadly.

"Well, it's about Auntie Jenny," Sarah continued. "Last week she was involved in a terrible car crash on her way to market. It wasn't her fault. This car came careering around a bend on the other side of the road and hit her. The other driver was badly hurt too."

"That's awful," exclaimed Tom. He had always liked his sister-in-law and felt guilty that he had not stood up for her more rather than get so involved with Mick. "Is she ok?" he enquired anxiously.

"No," Sarah told him. "She's in a coma in the hospital. Mum is worried sick. Gwilym is seeing to the animals for the time being. Mum goes to the hospital every time she is off duty. She is so worried, Dad. She's too proud to ask you to help."

"Thank you for telling me sweetheart. Let me think about the best way I can be of help. I will go and see Jenny. Let's hope she will be able to talk soon."

On his next day off, Tom went up to the hospital to see Jenny. There were no other visitors luckily. He was shocked to see the state she was in with tubes and machines attached to her. She lay very still and was as white as a ghost. Tom told the Sister in charge that he was family and she told him that Jenny had suffered a head injury in the crash, also had several broken ribs and had broken her right leg.

"She is lucky to be alive," the Sister told him. "We have operated to relieve the pressure on her brain and we are hoping she will come out of the coma soon. How much if any the brain has been damaged, we cannot tell yet." Tom was shocked to be told how poorly Jenny was. She had been through so much already. On his way home Tom thought hard about what he could do to help.

The next evening Tom went to see Gwilym. He desperately wanted to help in any way he could. Gwilym was surprised to see him.

"What can I do for you after all this time?"

Tom explained how he was very fond of Jenny and had only just heard about the car crash and that he wanted to help in any way he could. Gwilym relaxed a bit and his attitude became friendlier.

"Come in," He invited Tom into the house. "I'll put the kettle on." Over coffee Tom told Gwilym that he would hate for Jenny to lose her business.

"I know how she has worked and struggled over the years and her girls must be devastated."

"They are," Gwilym nodded. "They are coping as best they can. They see to the animals before and after college and I go down to see to the crops and pick the produce for the market but quite honestly with seeing to my own place as well the work is getting on top of me. It's too much. I'm no spring chicken." Tom smiled.

"I have a plan in mind if you will agree," he began. "By the way, whilst I was in prison, I took courses in horticulture and landscaping. Anyway, I've had a word with my boss. I told him the situation and he has agreed to let me work part-time for the time being. I could come over three days a week, the days before market and get the produce ready. I could see to the planting and weeding if that's ok with you?" Gwilym gave a sigh of relief.

"That would be a big help to us, Tom." Tom smiled.

"Glad to be of assistance. Let the girls know I will be over in the morning."

Cathie was pleasantly surprised at Tom's offer of help. He was true to his word and the produce left the smallholding and reached the market on time. The rent was paid and everyone was pulling together to help Jenny. Cathie sat by her bedside, talking to her at every spare moment, hoping that hearing her voice might be a breakthrough and Jenny would open her eyes and start to respond.

After three weeks had passed, Cathie was sitting talking and holding her hand as she had been doing constantly. Suddenly she was convinced that she felt Jenny's hand move in hers. She rang the bell to summon the nurse and sure enough Jenny was tightening the grip on her hand. Cathie waited anxiously for further signs and then she saw that Jenny had opened her eyes. She just stared and didn't seem to respond to her name. Cathie's nursing knowledge told her to be patient. It was too soon to tell if Jenny had permanent brain damage. She couldn't leave her side. By the evening Jenny seemed a bit more aware. She was still holding Cathie's hand and at last, she turned to Cathie and smiled. Cathie tried to speak calmly.

"Oh, thank God, "she whispered. "We thought we had lost you."

The ward sister gently pulled Cathie away.

"Let her rest and absorb what has happened," she advised wisely. "You go home now and get some rest. One of us will sit with her. You will see a different Jenny next time you visit," she smiled reassuringly.

From then on Jenny became stronger and more alert. The children visited every evening and gave her daily updates on what was going on with the smallholding.

"Gwilym and Tom have been marvellous, Mum," Dilys told her. "We might have lost everything without them. You mustn't worry about anything. Just get yourself better. Everything gets to market on time and we have paid the rent. Just you relax and read your magazines. You never have time to do that." Jenny laughed.

"That's true but I am not used to relaxing. I can't wait to get back home. But I am puzzled. Where does Tom fit into all this?"

"He's really stepped-up, Mum," explained Anne. "He comes over three times a week. He does the weeding and the watering and gets the produce ready for market. Then Gwilym runs your stall as well as his own." Jenny was very surprised.

"Well, I never. I knew Tom had taken up gardening but I never expected him to help us out like this."

"He thinks a lot of you, Mum," said Dilys. "I believe he is very sorry he didn't try and stop Dad hurting you years ago, so let's give him a chance."

"We will darling, It's all in the past. I am very grateful for his help now. The doctor says I can come home soon but I will still have my leg in plaster and my ribs are still very painful so I won't be much help around the place for a while yet.

"We all understand that Mum. You have to take it easy. We have it all in hand," replied Dilys. "We do the cooking; cleaning and the animals and Tom will see to the rest so you can just sit there and give orders." Jenny laughed,

"That will be a first. I will have to take every advantage of the situation."

The next week Jenny was back at home sitting in her favourite armchair. She had invited Tom and Gwilym over and with her advice the girls cooked a big roast dinner.

"I can't thank you both enough," Jenny told them. "I don't know how I can ever repay you.

"Well for me, we are friends Jenny, and that's what friends do. I don't expect repayment," replied Gwilym. Tom hesitated.

"I am thankful I was given an opportunity to make up for my cowardice. I knew Mick was treating you badly but my own wants overrode what I should have been man enough to do. I should have stood up to him years ago. I am so sorry." Jenny took his hand.

"Mick has paid the ultimate price for what he did. We should never have married but then I wouldn't have my two beautiful daughters, would I? Now we must put the past behind us and all move on." The girls nodded. Neither of them missed their father. They had grown up in an atmosphere of fear and violence and Mick had never spent any time with his children.

Jenny got stronger as the days passed and when the plaster cast was removed Tom drove her to physiotherapy appointments until she could get herself another van. They got along well. Tom continued to see his children every other weekend. The time came when Jenny felt she could manage the smallholding business again. Tom reluctantly felt it was time he moved back to Cheshire and take up his job full time again.

Chapter Twenty-Seven

He felt very alone. He loved his job but once his working day was over, he hated sitting all alone in his flat every evening. He had got used to the company of Jenny and the children. His curfew arrangements had been suspended so he started going down to his local, The Royal Oak. He needed company to stop him reflecting on what might have been.

He had come to accept that his plans of a reconciliation with Cathie was going nowhere. Cathie was always polite and chatty to him when the children visited, but he felt there was a wall between them that neither of them could break down.

One morning a letter dropped on the mat. He had an unexpected shock when he opened it. It was from Cathie's solicitor. She was applying for a divorce.

"Why Cathie?" He questioned her the next time she brought the children over. "I thought given time." She interrupted him.

"I have made my decision, Tom. It wasn't easy but my mind is made up. I am respected in the community now and feel I can't jeopardise my career. I can't trust you Tom. That's the bottom line."

"I thought I could earn your trust again over time," Tom pleaded.

"Well, I can't help how I feel, Tom. Also, it's not fair to keep you hanging on, hoping we can get back together. Perhaps now you can move on and find someone else."

That night Tom got very drunk. He was devastated. He had

believed that over time he and Cathie could renew their marriage vows and be a real family again. He made his way back to his lonely flat, cursing the day he had agreed to be an accomplice to Mick.

"I'm glad you're dead. You've ruined my life," he shouted up at the heavens as he staggered along the road.

The children stayed with him the following weekend and they helped to ease his depression. Like Cathie had experienced, he had to pull himself together for the sake of his children. He wanted their respect as a father even though he had lost Cathie.

He threw himself into his work, taking all the overtime he was offered, and his evenings were mostly spent down at the Royal Oak. He joined the darts team, played snooker and was soon accepted as one of the pub's regulars.

One evening a group of women came accepted appeared to be celebrating something. Tom noticed them as they were very loud, laughing and making lewd remarks to one another. One or two of them shouted suggestive remarks to the men playing darts. One pretty blonde woman in her early thirties kept catching Tom's eye. When he went up to the bar to order another drink, she followed him.

"Hi, you look a bit lonely, "she said. "We can have a drink together if you like."

Tom was a bit taken aback. It was years since he had been approached by a woman on her own. He hesitated.

"What about your friends?" he asked.

"Oh, that lot. They're a bit common, don't you think? Not my type if I'm honest."

And that's how it started. She introduced herself as Veronica. She was divorced with no children. She worked as a secretary for a law firm in Chester. Had her own place and drove a Mercedes convertible.

She's very pretty. Good figure, nice car, good job. What have I got to lose? My wife doesn't want me.

Tom and Veronica met up two or three times a week and, on the weekends when he was not seeing the children, they drove out to the Peak District or the Lakes and stayed over in nice hotels Tom felt as if he was alive again. She could never replace Cathie but Veronica was a good substitute. His divorce was still going through.

After six months he thought he would ask Veronica to move in together. He would have to look for a bigger flat or even rent a house. He could afford house. He would have to approach the children about the idea, but he was sure they wouldn't object. Neil was away a lot of the time with the Army and Sarah spent a lot of time with her friends at weekends. There was really only Paul to consider. He decided to go ahead anyway and ask Veronica.

Over dinner the following weekend Tom asked Veronica to move in with him. She agreed excitedly and they spent the next day looking at houses to rent. They found a pretty little cottage up a quiet lane on the outskirts of Knutsford and Tom put a deposit on it as soon as the estate agent opened.

Cathie had mixed emotions when she found out about Tom's plans. She was annoyed with herself that Tom's life still affected her emotionally. She tried to supress the pangs of jealousy that kept rising to the surface whenever she thought of Tom's arms around Veronica. She angrily suppressed these feelings, reminding herself of all the heartache Tom had caused her.

Tom and Veronica settled down to domestic life. He no longer felt the need to spend his evenings down at the Royal Oak, and only went out on darts nights. He was content to stay at home. Veronica was very homely and an excellent cook.

Paul liked Veronica, she made a fuss of him, but when the elder children came to stay, they were quite hostile towards her.

Tom tried to speak to them on their own.

"What is wrong with you? Veronica has bent over backwards to try to please you both. What's the matter? She is not trying to replace your mother."

"I'm sorry, Dad," said Neil. "Perhaps it's just seeing you with another woman. I'll try harder for your sake."

Sarah told Cathie about their feelings.

"She's too woman. I'll smiling and fussing over Dad. It's as if she's trying too hard. Can she be genuine? No one is that sweet and obliging."

"Well, it's your Dad's choice. We have to accept that Sarah. She won't affect us that much. You two have your own lives now and Paul seems to like her."

One Monday morning Tom woke up feeling a bit groggy.

"I don't feel like work today," he informed Veronica. "I'll phone the boss and tell him I'm not up to work today. I've got 'flu, I think. I'll take a couple of tablets and go back to bed."

"flu, have a good rest and I'll see you later," called Veronica as she left for work.

Tom didn't feel much better. Over the next few weeks there were days when he felt so tired and unwell. He began to struggle to do his job and his boss took him into the office.

"Are you all right Timed you need to see a doctor?"

"I'll be fine," answered Tom." It's just the 'flu lingering on I expect.

One Saturday he drove over to see Jenny. He often went to visit her and the children. Veronica always declined to go with him.

"You go and see your sister-in-law. She won't want me hanging around. I'll go into town and have a look around the shops. I'll bring you something back."

Jenny was shocked when she saw him.

"Ton, you've lost weight. Have you been to the doctor? You don't look at all well."

"I don't feel very well to be honest with you Jenny. I feel weak and so tired and sometimes I feel so sick.

"You must make an appointment to see the the doctor." Jenny's mind was racing.

What if he has got something really serious? Just as his life seems to be going well for him at the moment.

"Promise me you will make an appointment? Just to have a check-up please."

Tom nodded his head in agreement. He had to admit he was feeling a bit worse as time went on.

The doctor gave Tom a thorough examination and took some bloods. He couldn't give Tom a specific diagnosis.

"I'll give you a ring when the blood results come back," he told Tom.

A week later Tom was called back into the surgery.

"You told me you are not taking any tablets for pain. Is that right Tom?"

Tom nodded." I don't take anything. I've got cancer, haven't I?"

"No Tom you haven't got cancer but something puzzles me. Your blood results tell me you are taking tablets for pain control, but more than you should be over a twenty-four-hour period. The tablets are poisoning your system and your liver is badly damaged. That is why you feel so sick and tired. In fact, you are in liver failure and unless you come into hospital for bedrest and stop taking the medication you will need a transplant or you may die."

Tom looked blank. I am no junkie Doctor. On my children's lives I have not taken anything."

The doctor looked at him.

"Well, if you insist that you know nothing of this, I will have to look into it further. The police will have to be informed because you are slowly being poisoned."

As Tom was taken to hospital the police obtained a warrant to search his house. In the dressing table drawer in the bedroom, amongst Veronica's underwear they found numerous boxes of a pain-relieving drug.

On this evidence, as the drug matched what showed up in Tom's blood results, the police took Veronica in for questioning.

Tom contacted Jenny from the hospital with a garbled and bewildered explanation as to why he was in hospital and what the police had told him. Jenny rushed over to see him as soon as she had put the phone down.

"The doctor seems to think I will be all right," Tom assured Jenny. "My liver is not so badly damaged as to need a transplant. But I can't believe Veronica would try to harm me. I thought we were happy."

Jenny was puzzled. She broke the news to Cathie who was equally shocked.

"Whatever next is going to happen in that man's life He is going to be all right isn't he, Jenny?"

"Yes, he is Cathie. The doctor assured me that with lots of rest the liver will repair itself. I have asked him to come and stay with me to convalesce. But what about that woman Veronica? The police are still holding her. I don't think they believe she is innocent."

"The kids were right. They told me there was something about her they didn't like. They didn't think she was genuine. But why would she want to harm Tom?" asked Cathie.

"I'm no Sherlock Holmes. But we are going to find out." replied Jenny.

Chapter Twenty-Eight

Jenny went to the police station and enquired if they knew anything about Veronica's background.

"Not yet but we are working on it," she was told by the desk sergeant. "There must be a motive as to why she would want to harm your brother-in-law. As soon as we find out anything, we will let you know."

After a week had gone by, Jenny received a phone call from the police.

"We think we have found the motive and it's connected to your deceased husband." Jenny was puzzled.

"Apparently Veronica is the sister of a woman called Norma. Do you know her?"

"Oh yes," confirmed Jenny. "I know her all right. She was my husband's mistress, to put it politely."

"Well, we have interviewed her and she has confessed that it was all her idea. She and Veronica conjured up this plan to harm your brother -in-law because he gave the police information which eventually led to your husband being shot by the French police. It was all about revenge."

"Heavens above. That rat of a husband is still affecting our lives from the grave." Jenny had rushed over to give her sister the news. She carried on.

"That Norma is vicious. She must have been harbouring her resentment all this time. Well, she confessed to the police that it was her idea so they will both be charged. I don't think they meant to kill Tom, just make him suffer. But a jury might not see it like that. They'll certainly be sent to prison. What a pair of low-life."

"Well at least we have got to the bottom of why Veronica was poisoning Tom. I was worried sick about him. I was convinced he had something terminal."

"You still love him, don't you Cathie? Can't you let the past go? Don't you think he has suffered enough? He would jump at the chance to be with you again."

"The divorce is practically complete, Jenny. We just have to sign the Decree Nisi."

"Come on, Cathie, don't cut off your nose to spite your face. Swallow your pride. There's only been one man in your life, admit it. You have never bothered with anyone else over all these years.

Whilst Tom was convalescing on the smallholding, sometimes Jenny would invite Cathie and the children over for a meal or a picnic depending on the weather. Tom really looked forward to those times. He couldn't forgive himself for the foolish irresponsible way he had treated his family and had ended up in prison. Slowly he was trying to put those bad times behind him. He kept his dream alive that one day he would own his own landscaping business and earn the respect of his family again.

During these visits Cathie had begun to soften towards him but always in the back of her mind were the lies and deceit and of the awful time when she had nearly had to put her children into care. It was going to take a lot of mending. But as she sat in the sunshine, enjoying a meal with all her family, Neil was home on leave, and with Jenny and her children, all laughing and talking she took a moment to think to herself. 'Tom was my world once. Can he be again? I do not know. It's a long road back but maybe in time can I try to walk that road?'

Acknowledgements

I wish to acknowledge and to thank my long term partner, Alex, for his encouragement, for his reading of my early drafts and his helpful suggestions along the way. For his understanding that I needed time and space to write and edit *Web of Lies*.

I wish to acknowledge my children and grandchildren who always take an interest in my stories.

Finally, I would like to thank Karolina Robinson for her book cover design and Keith Abbott for his helpful advice in the publishing of this book.

A Message from the Author

Thank you so much for reading *Web of Lies*. I'd love to hear your feedback…

Email: sheilaantonie23@gmail.com.

Facebook: @antoniejohannson

You may like to take a look at my other books too…

Family in Need
by **Antonie Johannson** (pseudonym)

ISBN: 9781504994422 (softcover)
9781504994439 (hardcover)
and Kindle eBook
www.amazon.co.uk/dp/1504994426

Deception
by **Sheila Hall**

ISBN 9781976238512 (softcover)
and Kindle eBook
www.amazon.co.uk/dp/197623851X

Printed in Great Britain
by Amazon

75056488R00142